SHRUNK

Christopher Hogart

Bickerstaff Press
Cambridge, Massachusetts

SHRUNK

Christopher Hogart

You shall love your crooked neighbour
With your crooked heart

Auden

ISBN: 978-0-9883553-1-6 Softcover
ISBN: 978-0-9883553-0-9 eBook

This book is a work of fiction. Names, characters, places and events are either the product of the author's imagination or are used fictitiously. Any resemblance to actual persons living or dead, business establishments, events, locales, and or military names, units, operational events, are entirely coincidental.

Bickerstaff Press
Cambridge, Massachusetts

www.shrunkthenovel.com

The author would like to hear your comments on the book. Please feel free to contact him at chogart@shrunkthenovel.com

Printed in the United States of America

1

The dead raccoon outside the door of their house stirred in Henry and Helena Avalon feelings of repulsion and dismay. A dead animal at the door will disturb the staunchest heart. It jarred Helena's hopes and fantasies for the future. She was expecting, and Henry had set up his psychiatric office in the charming old house they had bought on Adams Street.

Had the creature that lay dead on their porch got there by his own locomotion and by coincidence lay down there to die? Had someone given to sinister gestures come onto their property at night and placed it there? The latter was unlikely, but still plausible. Wild animals, even those that crawl off somewhere when they know it's time to die, don't normally place themselves with care and precision in front of the door to a house. It was equally plausible, and implausible, that someone had deliberately placed the corpse there. If that had happened, the person responsible would presumably know them; but the Avalons were new to the neighborhood; scarcely anyone knew them, much less anyone who had had time to develop the sort of grudge that would inspire a person to leave a rotting carcass at their doorstep.

"You ought to visit the fortune-teller," said Helena,

who wanted to recapture her previously unclouded picture of the future. When she was anxious she did not like waiting and feeling helpless while nothing was said or done.

"Several of my friends swear by her. She looks the part, with her kerchief and a crystal on a round table. She takes herself seriously."

"Their livelihood depends on it. We have enough to do now with the house and other things," said Henry Avalon. A psychiatrist with an appointment at a prestigious teaching hospital, he had slight regard for soothsayers and the supernatural.

"I would think now is precisely when you want to see her, when so much that's new is going on."

They looked across the tree-lined street to the small park with its dark, green corners. It was a pleasant neighborhood, close to the city's center. One part of the picture did not conform with the satisfaction Henry felt and he lacked the power to eliminate it.

"Our neighbor's house looks sinister." They stood on the sidewalk in front of the two houses. "I don't like it being so close."

"I've scarcely seen him."

"It's hard to catch sight of him with so many trees and bushes growing up against the windows."

They looked at the dense evergreens and plants that covered the windows facing the street. Pieces of wood belonging to the fence that ran along the sidewalk had rotted and fallen out. Through the gaps one glimpsed a small over-grown area strewn with fallen pieces of wood and cracked concrete statuary – a derelict space, as much scrap yard as garden.

"Speaking of the devil . . ."

Their neighbor, Dr. Albert Prendergast, also a psychiatrist, walked up the street towards them on the way to his house.

"It's hard to feel comfortable around him – those eyes, and beard."

Prendergast's deep-set eyes lurked barely visible in the shadows beneath his brow.

"The Ayatollah of Adams Street."

Prendergast's tweed jacket and twill trousers, together with the beard, might have presented a picture of mature and benevolent middle age, an impression dispelled when he looked at you.

His arms hung still at his side and his head remained motionless atop his square frame as he advanced towards the Avalons, his eyes fixed on some point just to the side of them.

"We're thinking of extending the back of our house into the garden," said Avalon when Prendergast had come up to them. "Would you care to look at the drawings?"

Prendergast nodded and beckoned for them to follow him into his house. The three of them stood around drawings that Henry spread out on a cramped table in Prendergast's living room. The room was crowded with Victorian bric-a-brac and furnishings chosen according to the two aesthetic principles that they were old and made of dark wood. Old, regardless of color and design, was evidently sacred. A lamp shaded by stained glass shed a dim light. A stained glass panel hung in the window, conspiring with the bushes outside to limit the daylight that got in, and making it hard to see through the window even when the shades were up.

"I understand we're colleagues," said Avalon in an effort at conversation.

"Are you building an office?" said Prendergast.

"That's the plan."

"You could see your patients in your living room, as I do here."

"I hadn't thought of that."

"But you will?"

"I can certainly think of it."

"I suppose you ought to have what you want. It's nice to have an office in one's home. It's a good neighborhood, one of the last that hasn't been yuppified."

"It is a good neighborhood," said Avalon, glad to agree about something after having caught a whiff of struggle in the previous exchange.

"The former owner of your house and I thought of cutting down that big tree that grows across the property line, but we were both romantics. In the summer it provides shade for both houses."

"Romantics?"

"*She* was. The owner before her was something else. He would hover behind a window and, when anyone parked close to his driveway, run outside and make him move his car."

Avalon laughed. It was tempting to become an ally, to belong, together with his neighbor, to the small fraternity of those who, for the moment, laughed at the same thing, though he would not have laughed had he been alone. Prendergast's former neighbor did sound like a crank, and it is hard never to be gullible, to be suspicious of every piece of gossip. Avalon was new to the neighborhood, and there was no unifying principle like a shared scapegoat; harmless enough when the goat was long since gone.

"I gather you never saw *him* in your office here," said Avalon in an attempt to carry the conversation further.

"I wish I had."

"It is a peculiar profession, isn't it?"

Prendergast's eyes receded deeper into the shadows under his brow. "How do you mean?"

"It's not altogether different from something one would pay to do in an exclusive brothel," Avalon said, unable to resist a lame joke, "we take whoever comes to the door; people bring in their fantasies, except that with us they only talk about them; the client sets the agenda; and we're paid for it. It's not for nothing that it's called the second oldest profession."

"How did you acquire your practice?" asked Dr. Prendergast, sullen eyes looking down.

"Gradually, over time."

"Do your patients come in this weather?"

The remains of a late snowfall had made it difficult to get around that day.

"The weather is so often unpleasant. I'm looking forward to global warming. It's the only hope for New England. Even if it forced up the price of vegetables, it would be worth every penny."

"I don't think he enjoyed your joke," said Helena when she and Henry were in their house.

"I had the same impression."

"Don't you think there was something odd about the way he talked?"

"He may only have been trying to be tactful with someone he didn't know."

5

"Judging by the way he looked at you, I suspect that tact for him is nothing more than a syllable of tactic."

"He was quick to ask about my practice – pretty intrusive for someone we don't know."

"He may have his own peculiar sense of what's intrusive; he sees his patients in his living room. You may have said too much. You don't know what he's like yet."

"Should I be suspicious from the start?"

"No, but you joked with him and spoke with him as if he were an old friend. For all you know he has no sense of humor, and you don't know yet if he'll turn out to be a friend."

"I was made uncomfortable when he said that we ought to have what we want, as if it were up to him to allow it."

"I don't like his voice . . . it was oily and hard at the same time."

"Don't get me worried. We're going to have to live with him."

"Instead of wondering what it all means, darling, go and see the fortune teller. Her office is just a few blocks away," she added, when Henry appeared to dismiss the idea with a shake of his head.

2

A small red neon sign – *FORTUNES TOLD* – hung in the window of a one room street-level studio in one of the old, ramshackle houses on Arrow Street, directly across from the church. Avalon paused at the door and looked each way before going in, hoping that no one he knew had seen him.

He was uneasy in the fortune-teller's apartment and wanted to leave.

Along the wall a narrow single bed did service as a couch. The sparse furnishings and plate glass window looking directly onto the street made him think of prostitutes' rooms he had seen clustered in the vicinity of an ancient church in Amsterdam. Here too there was a church across the way. And here too the fortune-teller would deal with whoever came through the door. He had come to a corner of the city people visited when driven to deal with problems that were not readily solved in customary ways. At Avalon's request, the fortune-teller drew the curtain so that passers-by outside could not see in. She wore a long dress of brightly colored Indian cotton with a kerchief over her dyed hair. A crystal ball on an ebony stand rested in the center of a round table in the middle of the room.

"Seventy-five dollars."

She saw that Avalon paid reluctantly, as if he doubted that her services were worth it. When they sat down across the table from each other the fortune-teller took hold of his palm and leaned forward to examine it, then gazed into the crystal ball. Avalon held back until curiosity got the better of him. Then he too leaned forward and stared into the crystal. The fortune-teller took his palm again, not without noticing a fleeting moment when Avalon wrinkled his nose with contempt.

He was on the point of asking what she was thinking when she said:

"Nothing will ever happen to you."

"That's it?"

"You're lucky. If you're dissatisfied, you can always go across the street and pray."

No doubt some of her customers had done that, or come to her after they had been to church.

"No predictions?"

The fortune-teller shrugged.

"For seventy-five dollars – it's taken very little time, the hourly rate is considerable – I would like at least one prediction."

"If you insist: you will have difficulties at home."

"That's a safe bet, so many do. You don't take many chances. Do you have any advice?"

"Advice is less reliable."

"I'll have some anyways, thank you."

Her smile expressed venom and amusement in equal measure. "Love your neighbor."

3

The telephone call from Harold Mendelson, Director of Training at The Belair, one of Harvard's teaching hospitals, came that night as Henry and Helena were going to bed.

"Sorry to be calling this late. I was concerned that someone as virtuous as you might already be in bed."

"It's perfectly all right."

"At the last meeting of the training staff at the hospital, we thought it would be a good idea if you applied for a senior position that's coming up."

"I'm flattered. Thank you."

"It's not flattery. Your good work has not gone unnoticed. From your earliest days in training you were obviously one of our brightest. There are your publications too, inside and outside the field, and unfailingly intelligent comments. It's a committee decision, of course, and you no doubt have your enemies, as we all do, but I think you're in, and we'd be fortunate to have you with us."

"That would be very nice. Thank you."

"Good. Meanwhile, come to the retreat this weekend."

"It was Mendelson," Henry said to Helena when he had got off the phone.

"What was the conversation about?"

"One doesn't converse with Mendelson, one confers."

"What about?"

"I'm under consideration for a senior position at the hospital – a promotion."

"Oh, darling, that's wonderful, a feather in your cap, really!"

Henry did not respond, and Helena did not see in his face what she expected.

"You seem doubtful."

Distracted, Henry cocked his head to better hear a peculiar whistling sound outside.

"What was that?"

"I don't know."

"Do you think it was human?"

"Hard to say. It wasn't a tune. We ought to clear out some of the underbrush in the garden. It's attracted some wild animals."

"It sounded almost human."

"Who would whistle like that – and at this hour?

4

Cavendish College, rented for the occasion of the hospital staff's retreat, was a green place with lawns and woods and a pond about ten miles from Boston. Mendelson – who took pleasure in his mellifluous voice and carefully labored phrases, while getting lost in his paragraphs, was as graceful as a swan. He and Cobb welcomed the newcomers to their ranks.

They were there, in principle, to share their thoughts about the hospital and their profession. None of the junior staff had a critical thing to say; most, careful to avoid a misstep, said nothing at all.

More senior staff were less guarded. Mendelson and Cobb had both reached a point where their positions were secure. They had been colleagues for a decade. While Mendelson had built his career upon a new diagnosis, Cobb had worked his way up through the ranks with the obligatory two papers a year discussing others' research. He always had something to say, with little fear of disagreement or being questioned. He spoke at length of a new, more democratic era in the hospital and about the importance of input from all members of the staff. He and Mendelson let their thoughts about the future of the department be known to their polite listeners, the cleverest of whom were silently biding their time – perhaps for years – until they too would have the chance to give speeches and decide who got promotions.

At midday break Mendelson rose to speak. "Twenty per cent of the departmental staff's incidental budget is spent on the retreat. We may as well get the full benefit. It's time for Parson's Privilege."

The senior and junior male colleagues walked across a sleek green lawn to the edge of the pond at a secluded spot known as Parson's Privilege where, in the nineteenth century, college faculty, then entirely male, many of them members of the clergy, had granted themselves the privilege of swimming naked. The hospital staff disrobed, the more junior colleagues an article or two of clothing behind those more senior like Mendelson and Cobb. When they had been in the water and come out again and stood wet and naked on the bank, a boatful of laughing tourists, most of them women, sailed by a few yards from shore.

The doctors grabbed their towels and until the boat passed out of sight covered their genitals, all, that is, except Avalon, who covered his head, an oddity that did not go unnoticed.

"That was a bit peculiar," said Cobb.

"Some people are known by their faces," Avalon replied. "It's one reason why psychiatric theory has had to change."

Cobb laughed with the others, but found it hard to forgive Avalon for what he had said, and for not having said it himself.

*

Mendelson sidled up to Avalon after the break. "Would you mind co-teaching a course on the personality disorders with Cobb?" The course in question was usually taught by senior staff, or those on the way to joining their ranks.

As he made this offering to Avalon, Mendelson looked past him. He had a habit of looking beyond the person with whom he was talking to see if there was someone more important he might be talking to instead. When Avalon agreed, Mendelson went to find Cobb to let him know of the new arrangement. Cobb thought of saying something about Avalon to Mendelson, but decided it was premature.

*

Excited by the events earlier in the day at the retreat, including the success of his speech to newly promoted colleagues, Mendelson could not contain himself. He was too restless to stay in his house, which was situated in a more suburban neighborhood a mile to the west of the Avalons.

He stopped briefly to gaze admiringly at the colorful koi fish gliding effortlessly through the water of the small pond he had had built in his garden: "How graceful you are. I'd make love to you if I knew how." He liked to talk of love. An ordinary jog was not enough; his jogging clothes, except for the shoes, remained behind in a small heap on the closet floor.

The hill behind his house was covered with woods of birch and maple and crisscrossed by paths. Mendelson ran up and down the hill naked, avoiding the paths, enjoying thoughts about his increasing fame and professional stature.

*

That same afternoon, one of the brightest of the year with promises of a fine summer to follow, Helena Avalon gardened behind the house on Adams Street wearing a pair of red shorts, the Valentine's Day shorts she had worn at home for Henry on February 14. When Henry returned from the retreat she put the gardening implements away and they drove to the wood in the vicinity of Mendelson's house where they often took their walks. In the middle of the wood Helena stood still.

"Did you hear something?"

"Don't know; what do you think?"

"It was a rustling sound, like some animal. I saw something rush by."

"A squirrel, maybe."

"It was too big for that."

"There are raccoons here."

"Bigger than that too. It must have been the wind. I've become jumpy lately."

"There've been reports of coyotes coming this far into town."

"It was bigger than a coyote."

"The only animals that size this close to town are two legged."

"Why would anyone run there? The paths are a lot easier."

5

Looking out the window as she dried herself after a shower, Helena thought she saw, across the driveway that ran between her house and Dr. Prendergast's, a piece of paper and an article of clothing dangling in one of Prendergast's windows.

After putting on her glasses she saw *HOT RED SHORTS!* written with a marker on the paper. Below the sign hung a pair of red shorts, considerably larger than the pair she had worn in the garden.

She covered herself more carefully and pulled the window shade all the way down.

"Henry!"

She wouldn't raise the shade, but made Henry bend down to look through the centimeter left between the shade and the window frame.

"He might see us looking at him; in any case, I don't want him looking in."

"He must want us to look, or he wouldn't have hung those things in the window."

"It's an odd way to communicate."

"Oddly effective."

"And disturbing. I wish you would take this more seriously. It gives me the creeps."

"I'm sorry; it is creepy."

"And scary. Is there anything we can do besides pulling down the shades?"

"I doubt it . . . There is the First Amendment."

"This is becoming difficult for me."

"Shall I call a lawyer?"

"I suppose so."

Henry called Timothy White, a lawyer they had consulted about another matter some years before.

"I sympathize," said White. "You probably can't do much, other than ask him to take them down."

Helena was upset, but still clear: "Our encounter with the law leaves him free to do what he wants and us with no recourse."

*

That night, half an hour after Henry and Helena had turned out the lights and gone to bed, as if they were ready even in their sleep for it to happen a second time, they awoke to hear the same whistling sound they had heard the night before. It was too shrill and insistent to be made by any of the animals that came this far into town.

"There it is again," said Helena. "Do you hear it?"

"It woke me up."

"It has to be a person. Do you think it's deliberate?"

"But why? If it's deliberate it will have a purpose, and what could that be?"

"It's a respectable neighborhood with doctors and lawyers and the like. You don't expect anything like this."

"There are things so perverse that only a professional, well educated person with pretenses to intelligence could think them up."

Helena found the idea that the sounds were human intolerable and tried to revive her former belief.

"The night before we found the dead raccoon I heard what I could have sworn were the sounds of a wild animal in the middle of the night. Perhaps it's back."

"Let's hope so – it's the best possible interpretation."

"It makes me uneasy to think that a person's doing it. I don't know whom we could turn to."

"It's not the sort of thing one readily talks about. What would we say? 'Tell me, are there any wild creatures in the neighborhood who howl outside your house and leave rotten meat with the feet still on it at your doorstep?'"

"Let's not make it worse. Prendergast has a cat – but why would he be calling his cat at this hour?"

"He may call her when he goes to bed, and he may go to bed late."

Helena let herself be reassured and fell back to sleep.

6

"The problem is far more widespread than people think," Cobb said to the psychiatric residents in the course that Mendelson had set up for Cobb and Avalon to teach together at the hospital. "You will find that Gefühlsarmut, or Affect Deficiency Syndrome, is actually quite widespread, once you know what to look for. I suspect I have a touch of it myself. It's reasonable to think, with so many afflicted by it in some degree, that it may serve some adaptive purpose when it's not too severe, otherwise why would it be so prevalent? If it were always maladaptive, wouldn't those who had it have failed to survive in such numbers? Evolution and the principle of the survival of the fittest would have selected them out, purging the species of a perilous trait? We may want to make room in our thoughts, when assessing a patient, in addition to the usual considerations, whether in his psychological make-up he's too far to the other end of the spectrum, too much lacking in Affect Deficiency Syndrome, and missing out on its benefits. Would he lack the self-control of a person who is *not* swayed by his emotions? It is arguable that there may be something wrong with those who are altogether untouched by affect deficiency."

The residents for the most part gave Cobb their

attention. The bare, gray plastic walls of the room, the soundproofed drop-ceiling of synthetic fiber, the absence of anything else but chairs and a TV/DVD player on a bare metal stand, provided few distractions.

"It's true that he rarely shows much feeling," one resident whispered to another.

"When we first started, Mendelson and I . . ." Mendelson, some years Cobb's senior, and Cobb had been joint authors, a few years back, of a paper on Affect Deficiency Syndrome, one of a series of papers in which Mendelson had helped to popularize Affect Deficiency Disorder as a new diagnosis. ". . . it was a struggle getting the world to recognize the importance of this diagnosis. Now my practice is full; you needn't concern yourselves with sending me referrals." He gave the prettiest resident the mischievous glance of the successful man..

"I believe that even Koestler, our former department chairman, may have a touch of it," Cobb continued.

"Of course we want to be cautious, as with any diagnosis," Avalon interjected. Casually diagnosing colleagues like that went too far. Koestler had been his analyst. Avalon remembered that Koestler was affectionate with his wife and children, and had written a novel with a strong component of romance. If Koestler has Affect Deficiency Syndrome, he thought, I wouldn't know what it is, except material for articles useful in advancing a career. There could be good reason why Koestler might have been reserved with his feelings in Cobb's presence; Cobb had once said that he wouldn't mind eventually having Koestler's job.

"Even if a person has Gefühlsarmut," Avalon said aloud, "affect deficiency is a relative, not an absolute condition; as with other diagnoses, the rest of the person – which may be most of him most of the time – is an ordinary human being, and you'll want to find out what you can about him."

Avalon would have liked to engage the residents in an open discussion., but Cobb made it hard for others, including Avalon, who was supposed to be teaching the course with him, to say much, or be heard. While he spoke, Cobb busied himself with the unnecessary and noisy task of moving the television on its stand from one end of the seminar room to the other. Two of the residents smiled knowingly in Avalon's direction.

"How's the new seminar?" Mendelson asked when he ran into Avalon later in the day.

"It's mostly Cobb's show."

"Oh well; don't worry about Cobb. He's not much interested in personality, is he?"

"Odd that's the course he's asked to teach."

"I'm glad you're chipping in," Mendelson ignored Avalon's remark and patted him on the back, managing in a few sentences to condescend to several colleagues at once. "The residents have a lot to learn."

As he walked out of the hospital, Avalon felt the rush of freedom of a boy let out of school. Cobb had noticed Mendelson talking with Avalon. When by accident Avalon later crossed his path outside the hospital, Cobb turned away to make it clear to Avalon that he was snubbing him.

Avalon's "Hi!" reached Cobb's ears as the distance between them grew, prompting Cobb to ask himself: "Now, what does he mean by that?"

7

Prendergast had felt lonelier than ever since Avalon and his wife had moved in next door. Now and then he caught glimpses of them through their windows and felt the contrast between the domestic scenes he observed across the driveway and his own isolated existence in an empty house. Since the Avalons had become neighbors, he had taken to attending singles' events wearing fake crocodile leather cowboy boots.

On Friday night he persuaded a woman he met at one of them to join him in a stroll. It was a warm evening and Prendergast's house was on the way back to hers. She accompanied him as far as his house, planning to continue by herself. They lingered a while in the driveway that ran between Prendergast's house and Avalon's, Prendergast hoping that if the conversation went well she might come in.

"It's the first time I've been out with a psychiatrist," she said. "It must be terribly important work, to have someone's soul in your hands like that."

"I'm clinic director," said Prendergast.

"Did you hear that?" Avalon said to his wife in their bedroom above the driveway. "He writes scripts for addicts during the night shift at the city hospital. I suppose he's referring to that. They couldn't fill the job without giving it a title like Night Clinic Director. He's the only doctor there."

Helena and Henry, their lights off, listened to the dialogue below.

"I hope you cut your patients some slack," said the woman, thinking of her own problems.

"You have to be persistent if you're going to maintain control and prevail." Looking towards Avalon's house he muttered in a voice too low for her to hear him clearly: "not like him." Speaking audibly, he said, "The task, the skill, is to ensure finally that they do what you want."

"It is?"

"Why else should I be there? Why else would they be in treatment?"

"I doubt that's always easy . . . or desirable."

"It's a matter of how effective the psychiatrist is . . . You're going?"

"I'm afraid so. It's late. Thank you for walking with me."

Prendergast turned his back to her and pretended to take something out of his car until she disappeared from view. Looking up and seeing that Avalon's windows were dark, he blew the car horn. On the way into his house he rattled a trash bin, tilted it so that its contents fell onto Avalon's property, and entered his house.

"That was deliberate," Helena said of the horn.

"No, maybe not," she added hopefully. "His arm may have bumped against the horn accidentally."

"Don't you see what he's done with the trash bin?"

*

Half an hour after Henry and Helena had fallen

asleep, they were woken by the sounds of Prendergast repeatedly opening and slamming the trunk of his car, though he put nothing in it and took nothing out.

"Don't you think that's deliberate?"

"I'd rather not. He may have forgotten something . . . the first time."

After another half-hour, when Henry and Helena had managed to fall asleep again, they were awakened by the whistling sound they had heard a few nights before.

"Do you think he's calling his cat this time?"

"Cat's don't fly," said Helena, looking out the window. "He's standing on the second floor balcony, serenading us."

"What are we going to do if he does this every night?"

"I hope he's not ratcheting up? I dread to think what the climax could be. It's probably best to ignore him."

"Unless he's the sort who would punish us for not paying attention to him."

"He must know that we have no choice but to pay attention to him when he does this."

"Let's stop talking about it. I worked in the garden today; it has distinct possibilities."

They did not go back to sleep after that. Two days later Prendergast, who had seen Helena gardening, planted some small rhododendrons and azaleas he bought at a discount – poor specimens with an uncertain future – in holes he dug directly into the asphalt along the sides of his driveway, in the shade of the very large trees that grew on Avalon's property.

8

"I can't eat that," said John Waring, one of Avalon's colleagues. It was what he said about nearly every kind of food that makes life precious. He and Avalon were going through the buffet line in a restaurant in Harvard Square. Waring kept to his diet with the same intensity he brought to everything else, including leisure pastimes. Jogging was done with considerable huffing and panting; walking in a manner that strained him to the limit, forcefully kicking his legs out in front and swinging weights in his hands. He and Avalon lunched together every few months, formerly to talk about personal concerns, now as a gesture commemorating a withered companionship. Waring no longer had much time for such things; when they talked on the phone, even when they met, he would begin with: "I don't have much time . . . can't be long."

"If you touch that you have to pay for it," he said as Avalon's hand, en route to a roll, passed over a cookie.

"I wasn't going to."

The cookies, with unusual ingredients – like the rest of the food in this restaurant, dedicated to the latest beliefs about healthy eating – offered more to the eyes than the palate.

"I hear your star is rising," said Waring.

"News to me."

"Your name was mentioned at a party I went to last weekend. Mendelson said some nice things about you. He and Cobb are lightweights, you know. I've heard them present cases they had obviously got wrong. Since his book on quality control in psychiatry, Cobb isn't interested in anything else. He never fails to mention the subject and always finds it relevant." Waring was quick and hard with his judgments of men, but Avalon had not heard any judgments of himself and felt that he was still safe.

"In any case, I'm glad that what they say is friendly," said Avalon.

"I wouldn't be so sure it's friendship."

"I'd like to believe one can rely on there being limits to the scurrility and ill will of colleagues."

"If they think you're destined to join them, or will eventually hold some position of power, they'll make room for you. They'll drop you if they see your trajectory changes direction or you no longer want to be one of them."

"You're a bit cynical."

"It's better than being blind. You have to play the game if you're going to win."

"Mendelson's certainly been successful."

"His method for success is to promote a new diagnosis and ride it as far as he can. In the past he virtually took possession of Renault's Disorder; now its Affect Deficiency Syndrome, which he likes to call Gefühlsarmut Syndrome, after some wartime German who came up with the term. He sees it everywhere and he's got everybody else doing the same. One of the early papers was interesting; since then he's found a surprising variety of ways of saying the same thing."

"I wrote some of those early papers with him."

"I have a distant memory of your name on one of them. There was another name that regularly appeared as co-author."

"His mistress."

"Was she working in the field too?"

"She typed."

"Are you doing research now?" Waring spoke more quickly. The revived memories of Avalon's collaboration with a colleague as successful as Mendelson prodded him on.

"Had a project for a while, but had to ditch it. The statistics didn't work out."

"Make them," Waring said to be supportive; "everyone else does."

"Have you got something of your own cooking?"

"I'm doing some research. It's time for another promotion."

"What about?"

"Brain imaging, using fMRI brain scans."

"Imaging what?"

"I want to see what goes on in people's brains when they enjoy revenge, and to see how many of them otherwise have Affect Deficiency Syndrome."

"Affect Deficiency Syndrome? What would that have to do with revenge?"

"You have to go where the funding is. There's grant money now in Affect Deficiency Syndrome. I'll do your brain if you want – in the interests of science of course. But you can't eat beforehand."

"Why not? I wouldn't think it has anything to do with the GI tract."

"In order to get a base line, I image each subject's brain before and after showing them films of people wreaking revenge. In some there was no difference. At first I thought it was merely dross or, worse, data that invalidated the hypothesis. Then I found out that they had had a meal before coming in for the experiment. There isn't that much difference in brain activity between revenge and a good meal."

"Are they equally nourishing?" Avalon laughed. "I wouldn't want to think my brain was confusing the two," he said, thinking of his neighbor Prendergast.

"I still need subjects. I'll treat you to a good meal afterwards."

"No thanks. How are things at home?"

"Pam and I have retreated to our respective corners, and I keep myself busy, which helps."

Waring returned to his lunch. He chewed fast, another demonstration of how busy he was. Giving in to the temptation for any physician to discuss mutual patients he asked, "By the way, are you supervising a resident at The Belair who's involved in the Marston case?"

"The Marston case?"

"Their adolescent boy's been hospitalized again, the parents are all but separated although they live under the same roof . . ."

"Oh, yes. Are you involved?"

"I was, briefly. The mother came to me . . . wanted someone to tell her whether to divorce or stay married. When I wouldn't do that she drifted away."

"She doesn't know; she's empty," said Waring.

"I'm not sure what that means. Couldn't it be that she's constricted and depressed, can't express herself, or doesn't dare?"

"Maybe. If I remember right, it's a bad marriage. Perhaps they ought to separate."

"Consenting adults relate to each another in all sorts of ways. I sympathized with how difficult the situation must have been for her, but I had a holy dread of telling her what to do. She's the one who would have to live with the consequences."

Waring thought Avalon's position too virtuous and preachy, even prissy; he wanted to take him off his high horse, and saw an opportunity to boost his self-esteem at Avalon's expense.

"I doubt she understood your scruples or your reasons."

"Are you writing?" Waring thought it best to change the subject.

"Planning to."

"What about?"

"The mistakes we make with patients."

"That would be different. Everybody else is eager to demonstrate how expert he is. The rest of the world became more modest when Copernicus showed them that the world revolves around the sun. It's time our profession caught up."

"When they do, they'll compete to see how modest they can be."

"Who's cynical now?"

"Cynicism's not so bad. That reminds me, do you know the name of a lawyer?"

"What for?"

"Zoning matters, regarding the house and a crazy neighbor." He gave Waring a few details.

"What a situation! It provides you with an entire drama ready-made, though I doubt any dramatists would want him as a neighbor. As for lawyers, you could try Timothy White."

"He's the one I was thinking of. We consulted him once before."

"I'll be seeing him this afternoon about the divorce."

"Will you give him this when you see him?" Avalon took a rather good Barbaresco out of his bag and handed it to Waring.

"If he already knows you, I doubt he'll require a retainer."

"I know. But he was helpful once. It's to say thanks for that and hello again."

When they had left the restaurant Waring walked quickly with a forward tilt as though his center of gravity lay always a foot ahead of him. Avalon made an effort to keep up; beside Waring he felt clumsy and slow.

*

"The peace we offer is better than wine," said one of a group of Hari Krishnas in Harvard Square, who had spotted the bottle Waring was carrying. He wore a pale pink robe made paler by the blanched skin that looked as though it had been in water for a long time.

"That may give you a buzz," he persisted, "but not the true resonance."

Avalon, who found it harder than Waring to ignore signals coming from others, asked,

"Was he smirking?"

"I wasn't looking closely. They give me the creeps."

"Why?"

"These Hari Krishnas may seem benign and otherworldly, but you have to be careful with them; they're armed."

"I've never thought of them as particularly aggressive. I suppose their style invites some bullies and they've had some bad experiences."

*

Geoffrey Parsons, a student at Harvard, saw Dr. Avalon, his psychiatrist, a hundred yards off as he made his way through the Square. He had not yet settled on the topic for an assignment in his course at the university's Visual Arts Centre. He had been encouraged to do a piece of work with some local color in it. Reckoning that if his psychiatrist could do it, he could too, Parsons, more curious than Avalon, approached the Hari Krishnas.

"Are you a religion?"

"Not exactly."

"What's the difference?"

"It's not entirely different; we are devoted."

"Devout. That sounds like religion."

"Not devout. Devoted." The expression was firm now. It was evident, as it hadn't been before, that devotion did not require him to oblige this questioning student. His body resumed its sinuous wave-like undulations, but with less vigor, barely cutting the air, just enough to hint that Parsons was keeping him from his work.

"Devoted to what?"

Parson's questions had taken on the character of an interrogation, the Hari Krishna devotee did not feel obliged to cooperate.

"Our principles."

"I haven't seen you in the Square before. Are you sticking around, building a church?"

"We're not a church. But we're looking for a place in Cambridge.

*

At the end of the day Avalon left a message with Mendelson: "Thanks for everything. Lunch is good; we'll have a chance to talk."

On the way home he ran into Waring again not far from the Square on Prescott Street. Waring was on his way to his mistress's apartment with the bottle of wine that Avalon had asked him to give to Timothy White. Caught in the act, Waring felt compelled to say something:

"Honesty is the best policy: I gave Timothy a bottle of wine, one that's less refined than this one. Don't worry. He's an honest lawyer, but he has no taste. Something like this would be wasted on him. He won't know the difference."

"Why is it that whenever someone speaks of honesty, I'd rather not hear what he's about to say?"

Waring let that fly by and, lifting the bottle said, "I have absolute confidence in your taste."

"Should I have said, 'That's not the point,' or pointed out that he had managed to insult two friends with a single flip remark?'" Avalon reflected as he walked away. He shrugged. It wouldn't have made a difference.

*

In his mistress's apartment, Waring received a call from Cobb. Before it was quite over he said, "Avalon can have a sharp tongue."

"He does, doesn't he? We'll have to watch that."

"It's too bad. He could be quite successful otherwise."

"You have good taste in wine," said Waring's mistress. "One of your many admirable traits."

"Thank you." Waring welcomed the compliment, and sincerely enjoyed it. Having taken possession of the bottle, he accepted the compliments that came with it.

*

That night, half an hour after the Avalons had turned out their lights, as they were falling asleep, Prendergast rattled a trash bin and slammed his car door three times making as much noise as he could. He went inside to his kitchen, which was lined with heavily lacquered pine cabinets, bent down between the plants that grew better around his kitchen sink than in his garden, and brushed his teeth. After making himself a warm drink, he went upstairs, to his bedroom – stepped onto the balcony and whistled shrilly, angrily, insistently.

"Perhaps you ought to have a *tête a tête* with him," Helena suggested.

"A *tête à bête* would be more like it. I doubt it would do much good. He makes sounds up and down the line of his territory rather like an animal leaving his scent than a man who wants to talk."

"His bark may be worse than his bite." When Henry laughed she added: "Some clichés are made by the truth."

32

"Go, if you think it's a good idea. If the trouble between us is a male-male thing, you'll have better luck."

Helena put on some clothes and went to knock on Prendergast's door.

A gravelly voice behind the closed door said: "I'm not Dr. Prendergast."

"I'm not Mrs. Avalon."

Prendergast opened the door and stared at her before he said, "Why do you put up with that nut?"

"I'm not sure I agree with your characterization of my husband."

"I see; you're with him. That addition you're building is going to be a massive structure next to my property."

"It's only one and a half stories high," Helena tried reasoning with him. "It could have been two stories like the rest of the house. Your garage is a bigger structure. If you have any suggestions, though, we'll be glad to hear them. Come to the meeting of the Zoning Board next week. Meanwhile, please let us sleep."

*

"I tried," Helena said to Henry when she returned to the house. "I've observed a pattern of behavior for a while now that worries me. I wore red shorts; he hung a pair in the window. The day before yesterday I did some gardening; yesterday I saw him gardening, if you can call it that. I watered our plants; he got his wet. Which makes me think : you and I live here together – if he had a woman . . . ?"

"We could place a personal ad for him: *"WSM of*

strong character seeks meek, tolerant masochist who will let him have his way with her and admire him for it."

Prendergast stepped onto his balcony and whistled again.

"WSM who enjoys late nighttime revels . . ."

"I can't imagine him enjoying anything but the sort of thing he's been doing."

"We'll see." Avalon played a few notes on his flute next to an open window.

Moments later Prendergast whistled loudly and angrily and slammed the balcony door shut.

"Now you're whistling to each other," said Helena. "How romantic."

"It's hard not to. The true golden rule is: you will do unto others what is done unto you."

"Sorry for the sarcasm. What I meant was that we're probably his most passionate relationship, perhaps the only one."

"I'm not yet ready to laugh at this, but I'm not above trying to do something. What do you think of: *'Offbeat WSM professional and property owner with a taste for music and nightlife...'"*

"That's better. We'll bounce it back and forth with e-mails tomorrow. When we've got it right, we'll send it to Boston Magazine."

*

An hour later, when Henry and Helena had slipped into a sleep too deep to be disturbed, Prendergast hung the Red Hot Pants sign in the window again, wolf-whistled, and slammed his door. It vexed him that there was no reply, that his efforts had been futile. He felt it as something akin to rudeness or coldness on their part.

"Won't he think it odd when women contact him saying they're responding to his ad?"

"He may wonder a bit about what's going on, but he's probably so hungry for a date he's not going to turn them away."

*

Walter Tremolo, sitting on a bench in the small empty park across the street from both houses, heard the sounds coming from them. He was in the habit of wandering the city at night taking still and video pictures – he had accumulated a considerable archive – and often sat in the park on Adams Street to enjoy the dark quiet of the place, disturbed this evening by the sounds from across the street. He dutifully turned his camera in the direction of the disturbance, though it was too dark for him to know what he might catch on tape.

The following day Henry placed a personal ad in Boston Magazine.

9

"He says 'we'll have a chance to talk'. That sounds as though I'm expected to listen to some spiel of his," thought Mendelson as he listened to Avalon's message. "What would it be? A complaint? A Request for some favor? I've done enough for him."

He was aware of having treated Avalon brusquely at times, but considered that a small point; his own growing importance made it inevitable that he would have less time for some of those he already knew. Besides, he had recently taken the trouble to let Avalon know that he had been promoted.

"Who is he," thought Mendelson, forgetting that he had suggested the lunch, "that *I* should listen to *him*."

Flushed with the news of his own promotion a few years ago Mendelson had said, "It's nice to run with the big boys."

Avalon had half-jokingly answered, "The risk in running with the big boys is that you remain a boy, with the goals and ideals of the schoolyard, and the belief that whatever big boys do is what every boy should aspire to."

For Mendelson there was no free lunch, nor free insult either, not even an imagined one. He persuaded a secretary at the Belair Hospital, where he had dropped by for a consultation, to leave a message with Avalon canceling their lunch.

*

Avalon lunched alone before the afternoon meeting of the Cambridge Zoning Board. He was anxious about the meeting, and eating in the café across the street from City Hall, where the city politicians ate, didn't help. Businessmen were there who sought the help of the Zoning Board in extracting an extra hundred thousand dollars from one property or another. For that they needed a variance they hoped would be granted because of their connections with men who thought and looked like themselves and who worked in and around City Hall and did business with one other in the café across from City Hall and, for the most part, spoke with the same abrasive accent. They were men who might have secured a place in the state legislature, and sometimes did, but would probably have failed had they tried to be elected to Congress; it would have been difficult to overcome the impression of small time wheeler-dealers. The art on the walls of the café was the sort that Woolworth's would have sold if it were still in business a few blocks away in Central Square; the dust on the frames suggested they might once have come from there. Suspicious of how off-putting the food might be, Avalon went through the menu carefully and selected a turkey sandwich as the one item that would be hard to spoil. He was wrong. The look and taste of the meat raised questions about what had been done to the turkey to turn it into the damp, glistening slices that lay between the limp pieces of tasteless bread he held in his hand. He scolded himself for being so critical; he would be less likely to present his case well to the Zoning Board if he were in a crabby mood. Helena joined him in time for a coffee that was too acidic and upset his stomach. They crossed Massachusetts Avenue together for the meeting that was to be held in the hearing room in the City Hall where Timothy White was waiting for them by the door.

Copies of the plan for the addition to the house lay on a long table in front of the members of the zoning board. They seemed willing to grant a variance and, despite a few questions, all went smoothly until Prendergast rose to speak. Different people see the same things differently. It seemed to Avalon that no one else saw the similarity between the eyes that looked out accusingly from the bearded face of an ayatollah and the smoldering anger with which Prendergast's eyes gazed out from under his brows at a flawed world, or they would have taken more care in responding to what he asked for.

"I'm Dr. Avalon's immediate neighbor. The addition to his house that you see in these plans – plans I haven't seen until now – will affect me directly. Such a massive structure will cast a considerable shadow over my yard."

"Actually, I did show Dr. Prendergast the drawings," said Avalon when Jeremy Smith, the chairman of the board, pulled his half-moon glasses down his nose and looked across the table in his direction. "They're for a structure only one and a half stories high, half a story lower than the rest of the house."

Avalon whispered to Prendergast, "Why did you say you hadn't seen the drawings? They're the same drawings we showed you in your living room."

Prendergast waved his hand dismissively. "There

are lots of considerations in a matter like this."

"Meaning it's all right to lie?"

Timothy White leaned close to Avalon and muttered to his client, "What he said could seriously prejudice the Zoning Board against you."

"It's not true."

"Doesn't matter."

"Are you opposed to the Board granting Dr. Avalon a variance?" Jeremy Smith asked Prendergast.

"I wouldn't want to stand in the way of Mr. Avalon getting what he wants. If he were to construct a fence between our properties . . ."

"'That's a hundred feet of fence," said another member of the Board, a woman who had recently built a shorter fence and thought that what Prendergast wanted was a lot to ask for.

"Not that unusual," said a rotund man who wore a casual shirt open wide at the neck and a short, windbreaker jacket – also a member of the Board. "It sounds like an appropriate way to resolve the problem."

"What is the problem?" Avalon demanded.

White again tilted his head close to Avalon's to say something privately to him. Before he could, Avalon said to the Board. "There's already a fence there."

"He wants a new one." White whispered. "And he may get it. You ought to know that the last Board member who spoke owns a fencing company."

"Isn't it a bit corrupt that he should be sitting at this hearing?"

"Be careful, you're being railroaded."

"In the interest of good neighborliness . . . ," said the Board member who was the proprietor of a fence making company.

"Do you mean that I have to prove I'm a good neighbor," Avalon interrupted, "and that the way to do that is to build him a new fence at my expense simply because he wants it?"

"Would you expect Dr. Avalon to pay for the entire fence?" asked the woman on the Board who was sympathetic to Avalon.

"I could contribute something," said Prendergast.

"Good," said Jeremy Smith, who looked at Avalon over his glasses and bow tie. "I ought to say, in the interests of full disclosure, that I'm a friend of Dr. Prendergast, and probably shouldn't be involved any further. We'll leave it that the two of you will sort out how much each of you will contribute."

So it was left that a fence would be built, without specifying precisely what sort of fence, or in what proportions Avalon and Prendergast would pay for it.

"He's a friend of Prendergast!" Avalon said to White. "He waited until after he'd conducted the meeting to make a grand gesture of acting properly in recusing himself. Why didn't he remove himself at the beginning? The whole process is pretty dubious."

"You're right, of course. For another fifteen thousand dollars you could take the matter to the state Superior Court, where you would probably win and get the Zoning Board's decision reversed, no cost to the Board. A fence will be less expensive."

"Then justice is a matter of how much money you've got to spend."

"Sometimes it's like that."

10

"How much money is this going to cost us?" Avalon asked as he and Helena walked home. Stung by his helpless position in a losing game and anger at having lost it, he felt his blood coursing through his temples, and a serious erosion of whatever hope was left that something could be worked out.

"He said he would contribute."

"That means we'll have to have further dealings with him."

"Oh, Look!" Helena was suddenly excited. "It's worked!"

"What has?"

As they stood outside their house, Prendergast walked towards them in the company of a woman the Avalons had not seen before.

"The ad," Helena whispered. "It's worked! Perhaps he'll calm down now."

As Prendergast and his new friend passed by, he whistled, his shrill and hostile way, the same bar of notes with which he woke them up at night.

"There he goes with love on one side and hatred on the other; it's hatred that's his true passion, that inspires his music."

*

The sounds heard by the Avalons emanating from Prendergast's house were different that night.

"I like the noise," said Prendergast as he made love to his new friend, pinning her arms as if they were tied down, an arrangement in which she obliged him, though she had initially tried to embrace him.

"The ad is working," said Helena. "It's awful that we have to wish him well in this."

"Why should we wish him well?"

"If he's happy he may leave us alone."

"We'll have to see. Dealing with the opposite sex doesn't always calm a person down."

*

Prendergast's harassment of the Avalons intensified during the following weeks. In the hope that if he got what he wanted he might finally be appeased and leave them alone, Avalon hired men to build a hundred feet of fence six feet high. The first two communications to Prendergast regarding the contribution he had promised at the meeting of the Zoning Board went unanswered. After the third time, Prendergast replied with a letter that dispensed with a greeting and had no signature at the bottom.

> You will construct a new 12-foot-high fence the length of the line between our properties (approximately 100 feet). The composition of the fence will consist of ten feet of flat board topped with two feet of lattice. It will be

completed in two weeks' time, during which I will inspect it to see that it is being built properly according to these specifications. For each day beyond the first day of construction the project is delayed, and for any detail in which it fails to meet specifications, I will deduct $100 from my contribution (the amount of his contribution had never been specified).

This was a bit much. Avalon telephoned the office of the Zoning Board and was told that anything above six feet could be considered a spite fence and required special permission from the Board. Avalon instructed the workmen to proceed with the installation of a fence six feet high along the length of the line between the two properties.

11

"Cobb and I were talking the other day." It was Mendelson on the phone. He had had misgivings about his harsh thoughts about Avalon the other day. The literary group gave him an opportunity to smooth things over and still keep his distance.

"Would you like to join a group of us who meet once a month to talk about books? I can only attend one more meeting; the group could do with another member. Literature isn't our field, but some of our colleagues read and I hear you're one of them."

"I'd like to very much, thank you."

"It would be our good fortune. It's a kinder, friendlier hospital staff these days, now that the new generation is no longer wedded to the old orthodoxy and not so relentlessly hierarchical."

Cobb and Mendelson, who were in their fifties, liked to present themselves as a members of a new generation and advocates of change.

"I've heard a number of compliments lately," Henry said to Helena when he was off the phone. "When you reach a certain point in the game, the atmosphere changes. It's like becoming a senior at school."

"And joining a mutual admiration society."

*

The positive effect of the news from Cobb lasted no more than a day. Two hours into the night's sleep, Henry and Helena were awakened by the sound of Prendergast throwing rocks against the new fence that separated their properties.

"Turn on the cam-recorder."

Henry fumbled in a drawer, looking for it.

"It's on the window sill,' said Helena. "I put it there last week."

Henry turned it on and leaned out the window.

"Why are you doing this?" he shouted down.

"Because you're a vile, disgusting person."

"We built you a fence. What more do you want from us? Why are you throwing rocks? You'll damage it."

"Faggot! That's not the fence we talked about." Prendergast hurled another rock, loosening another plank in the fence, then threw himself shoulder first against the fence with the full weight of his body to separate more planks from the cross boards they were nailed to.

"'We talked about?' You mean there was another kind of fence you fancied and you're furious because we didn't do everything you demanded precisely as you wanted it, regardless of the cost to us, regardless of whether we were obligated to do it, and despite you're not having contributed as you agreed you would. You're lucky we've done as much as we have."

Another rock slammed against the fence, dislodging the upper end of another plank.

"Faggot!" Another stone was thrown.

"We've got him now," said Henry, pointing to the camera when the rampage stopped.

"Knowing that may help us get back to sleep now."

Half an hour after they had fallen asleep, they woke again when Prendergast whistled and then, to make sure of the job, went downstairs to blow his car horn. Henry was now too angry to sleep. The thought that he had caught Prendergast's actions and words on tape mitigated his anger; still, it was dawn before he had the chance to catch another hour's sleep before the alarm.

He went directly to the camera.

"Shit!" he said, looking at what he had on tape.

"What's wrong?"

"We didn't get him. There's an hour of nothing happening and then it goes blank."

"I turned it on when we went to bed," said Helena. "I'm sure of it."

"I must have turned it off when I thought I was turning it on."

The blank film was a devastation.

"I think about the creep all the time now. I feel so helpless. It's like a dream from which we can't awake. It doesn't matter what we do. He treats us the same way regardless. He draws us out of our own world and into his; it's like something happening in science fiction."

Helena's face, normally placid and graced with smiles that came easily, was tense and earnest.

*

When they examined the damage in the morning light they found that a plank dislodged from the fence had been removed and now occupied the same place in front of their door as the dead raccoon had.

"Oh God, Henry, look!" Helena pointed to several places where their car was badly scratched.

"Do you think the car provokes him, like a bull, because it's red?"

"He is as territorial as an animal. I'm surprised he doesn't pee up and down the property line."

"He sends all sorts of things over it."

It was a while before Henry could speak again. Deep within his being he felt a helpless urge to violence tearing him apart. "There's nothing obvious that we can do about it; the temptation to violence is overwhelming. I can see how the Mafia got started."

"Promise me you won't do anything violent with that man! You and your honesty and reckless pride. You'd be reacting to him; he would be following his plan, and you'd become part of it. He would have all the advantages."

12

"Whenever I see the letters m-e-r in a French work," Jane Bruckner was something of a hostess for these literary-psychiatric gatherings and liked to talk at them, "I find it terribly suggestive: *la mer*, the sea, *la mère,* mother, *mer*maids . . ."

"Yes," Cobb nodded.

"That's good," said Mendelson.

The three of them often agreed.

The importance of what Jane Bruckner said and its relevance to what they had been talking about was unclear to Avalon. He assumed that there was no harm in contributing something himself.

"Part of the charm of his books," he said of Stendhal a few moments later when they got back to the author they had been talking about, "is his style. It's not all that different from his journal – as if he's talking to a friend. We're drawn into his world as if we're included among The Happy Few to whom he dedicated *The Charterhouse of Parma*. I wonder if he believed he was one of them. All movement forward into the future is blocked in the world he describes in *Charterhouse*."

An expression of distaste flickered across Cobb's face. He wanted Avalon to shut up. It was evident by now that Avalon knew more about the evening's topic than he did. Bruckner and Mendelson also hadn't read Stendhal's journal and did not appreciate Avalon's mentioning it. When Mendelson had invited Avalon to join this group of colleagues who met to talk about books he hadn't known that Avalon had any particular familiarity with them. Until that moment he had regarded Avalon as junior to himself, akin to a younger sibling. He would have preferred to continue to think of him that way, but no longer could. Cobb felt offended and belittled by Avalon's knowing what he didn't know and hated Avalon for his role in making him feel that way. He could not have acknowledged this to anyone, not to Mendelson, not even to himself. He needed another basis for his dislike of Avalon. His first try was not very successful.

"In my student days," Cobb said, "it was generally believed that one shouldn't consider the author when talking about a book. The text was the thing."

"There was a time when people argued that," said Praeger, a literary academic who had been invited to join them that evening, whom the rest looked to as an authority. "It led to some pretty sterile critical work. In Stendhal's case, especially, given what we know about his life from his journals and how much of it figures in his work, it would be willful blindness."

Praeger's defense of Avalon did him no good; Cobb's dislike of him intensified. He consoled himself that if he couldn't put Avalon in his place tonight, he would have occasion to set things right another time. Until then he would do what he could to eliminate a problem he had helped to create for himself.

"I suggest that the group not meet for a while," he announced at the end of the evening. "I won't be able to

49

come to any meetings for a few months, not until after spring, and no one meets in summer.

"We won't meet at all?"

"The group can meet without me," Cobb went on, knowing they wouldn't; the meetings had been his idea. "If not, perhaps we can start again next autumn." By that time he might be able to arrange things so that Avalon wouldn't be one of their number.

"I liked your remarks," Praeger said to Avalon on the way out. "Would you like to join me on a paper on the psychiatrist's style?"

"I'd be interested in that."

"Will you be coming to the meetings in the spring if we have them, or next autumn?" Avalon asked Jane Bruckner as she was leaving.

She said nothing and turned away. Under the gleam of a well-dressed presentation, she was hot tempered and quick to hate. She had talked as much as anyone that evening, more than most, but did not like someone else talking as much as Avalon had unless he was her senior.

"Interesting," Waring said to Cobb as the group dispersed. "Avalon knows a thing or two."

"He doesn't know the first thing about people's feelings." Cobb enjoyed the virtuous breezes on the high horse he had just mounted almost as much as having Avalon underneath the hooves.

The human currents flowing from the room, carrying the members of the group along as they filed out of the building, brought Avalon up beside Cobb.

"We're not meeting next month, then?" Avalon asked.

"I'll be on vacation,"

"Where are you going?"

Cobb dropped his head and did not answer. Until that evening, until a few minutes ago, though with some reluctance, he had regarded Avalon as an up and coming member of the profession who would very likely become part of the unofficial inner circle; what had happened this evening caused him to pull back and be silent. His implacable hatred, for which he had just found a virtuous rationale, was not the sort of thing he could mention to Avalon; at the same time he couldn't say anything else.

As Cobb and Waring said good night to each other, Avalon tried to say good night to both of them, but before he could get the first word out, Cobb, with the exaggerated, jerky movements of someone too angry to control himself, abruptly turned away, tilting his head up in a snub too obvious to be mistaken, an exaggerated gesture that bore resemblance to what one might see in a cartoon in *Punch*.

"You want to be careful," Waring said to Avalon when Cobb had left. "You could acquire a reputation."

"A reputation for what?"

"As someone who goes too far in displaying what he knows, showing off, too intellectual . . . something like that."

"Did Cobb say something?"

Waring didn't answer, unwilling to acknowledge that he had been Cobb's willing messenger.

"I don't understand why he would say that," said Avalon. "I talked because I was interested. Praeger asked me afterwards if I would like to do a paper with her; Lazarus too was interested in what I said. I don't see that anyone's feelings were hurt except Cobb's, if that's what happened. I'm sorry if they were, but I'm not sure how much it's my problem or his."

"That's the way I see it too," said Waring, eager to agree and scurry away. He said it without the intensity with which he had conveyed Cobb's criticism, too quickly for it to have a reassuring effect. Waring generally thought it not rude, but manly to be abrupt, the necessary consequence of a busy life; now there was an additional reason to keep their conversation brief.

It was a lonely drive home for Avalon. He failed to appreciate the graceful line of the park along the lagoon. He had been stung by what had happened in the latter part of the evening, tossed between resentment and anxiety about its possible long-term implications, and a new pessimism about a future, that so recently seemed within his grasp, of increasing congeniality among colleagues. They were intense feelings of the sort that are hard to deal with alone, but that one doesn't like to talk about.

Intense feelings of any kind, good or bad, are tiring, and he arrived home exhausted. He picked up the unfinished paper in which he was reworking some classical theory – theory couldn't hurt his feelings – and wrote, perhaps in reaction to the bruising experience of the evening: "The phallus is a perfectly good phallic symbol, but may symbolize other qualities, even nurturance . . ." Theory was no help to him that night.

*

With cunning patience, Prendergast waited until the lights in the house next door had been out a while before he went down to his car and blew the horn, slammed the door, then whistled loudly as he walked back inside his house. Such disturbances occurred irregularly, but frequently enough that the anticipation of them made the Avalons light sleepers, easily awakened even by the lesser noises Prendergast made to disturb them. Once awake, their anger and their helplessness, and the prospect that Prendergast's harassment would continue indefinitely, made it hard to return to sleep.

"I don't know how long I can take this," said Helena.

"His whistle is the sound of the pure aggression of a creature of prey announcing his intention to do us harm."

The next morning Helena saw that one of the tires on the car was damaged beyond repair.

"He slashed the tire under the baby seat," said Helena, more than usually upset.

She had bought the seat in anticipation, nurturing fantasies that were part of her preparation for the baby's arrival. It felt as though Prendergast had slashed her fantasies along with the tires.

"White says that someone this crafty probably won't go too far, if for no other reason than to avoid getting into serious trouble."

"It may not get *him* into trouble; I was thinking of us. He crossed a line when he slashed that tire."

"He did."

"Don't you think we ought to move?"

"I'm sure that's what he wants."

"What if he does?"

"With broker's fees and moving expenses, it would cost upward of a hundred thousand dollars to move, not to mention the capital gains tax. Is it worth that much just to get away from him? Sooner or later he should get tired and calm down."

"I don't want to wait for that, not with the baby coming. I want to move."

"Meanwhile, life goes on. Here, you'll need this." He gave her a check for her tuition; she was acquiring post-graduate credentials for a career as a laboratory scientist. "You'll feel more independent when you've got the degree, less vulnerable.

"I don't follow. What's the connection between feeling more independent and dealing with the creep next door? That's not why I went back to school."

"It will make you feel better won't it, and that will make you more resilient."

"What you say makes me uneasy. You're thinking in ways which imply that we're staying here regardless of what Prendergast does."

What she said was true enough; Henry was not ready to think seriously about moving. He did not reply.

13

It had been some time since Avalon had seen his mother, long enough to feel sufficiently guilty to pay her a visit. He thought it unfortunate that guilt was such a powerful motivator but, aside from that, there was always a chance that he might find some comfort with her and enjoy her company in a way that would remind him of a time –he had trouble remembering it – when he believed he had felt safe with her in a way that eluded him now.

"You're looking better," she said as he walked into her apartment.

"You say that every time you see me."

"You ought to be glad I don't say something else."

The bright daylight outside was no more effective in reaching him in his mother's apartment than the uncertain memories he had tried and failed to retrieve. The walls were painted green according to a Victorian belief, shared by Mrs. Avalon, that the color was soothing, suggestive of green gardens. They did a poor job of reflecting incoming light and made the colors of the interior less vibrant.

Eighty years had not softened Mrs. Avalon's features; whatever she was going to do she would do with determination, a trait that had sometimes provoked defiance in Avalon but had more often intimidated him. The yearning for a comforting tenderness was far from consciousness now, safely hidden where it was unlikely to be remembered, and disappointed.

His mother's faculties had begun to fail, causing abrupt fluctuations in several functions, though her readiness for a rejoinder had been spared. In a moment of senility she asked:

"How are you doing in school?"

Seeing no reason not to profit from the occasion, Avalon replied, "Better than most of my classmates."

In a momentary return to clarity she looked at him incredulously. "Oh my! Then how are they doing?"

It was too good a day to remain indoors. Once they might have gone out together for a walk; today Avalon went by himself. He crossed the Common and came within range of the church from whose open windows he heard a choir sing a Bach chorale that promised to soothe the soul. He stepped inside the church and sat down.

He even liked the sermon by the minister, Arthur Winfield, who held a chair at the university as Professor of Moral Values. The pews were far enough apart to stretch one's legs. Large windows afforded an ample view of the green, sunlit world outside. The combined effect was so pleasant he thought that he would leave ten dollars in the collection plate when it came round.

"We can not always know finally what is good for mankind," Winfield intoned. Men of religion, when doing their job, rarely use an ordinary voice. "We must keep in mind the validity of values different from our own, the ultimate benefits of allowing the music of life to be played on a full keyboard."

"'Life played on a full keyboard' . . . a suspicious phrase," thought Avalon. As Winfield spoke of the value of beauty and passion, Avalon remembered Prendergast's red face aflame with passionate hatred.

"As much as anything else, things that move us emotionally, even physically," Winfield's resonant, honeyed voice reached to the far corners of the church, "like the ethereal beauty of poetry, or a lovely face, should be welcomed as gifts from a bounteous divinity."

The large windows of the church were open. Life from the warm, green world outside drifted in, including flies and bees, drawn by the bright colors of the clothing of some of the congregation which they mistook for flowers, and perhaps by the shade of the interior. The interior of the church grew warmer as the sermon grew tedious, while all that made life beautiful was increasingly to be found outside. Winfield had left by the door a box for contributions to support the world-wide promulgation of his cause – "The Growth of Tolerance and Pleasure For All At Home & Abroad." On the way out of the church Avalon dropped a piece of paper with some verses on it from Keats: *Beauty is truth, truth beauty – that is all / Ye know on earth, and all ye need to know*, into the open box– and took from the box a five-dollar bill.

Despite a professionally trained insight, he did not ask himself if his behavior leaving the church had anything to do with his earlier encounter with his mother. It was his day off. There was no reason he could think of to justify painstaking introspection on this fine morning that he reclaimed for himself as he left the church. He would not willingly have talked to anyone just then about his feelings regarding the day's experiences, not to mother, nor minister, nor analyst.

*

Nor did it to occur to him on Monday that his experiences of the day before had anything to do with an exchange with his patient, Geoffrey Parsons.

"I'm fed up," said Parsons. "It all feels so static, nothing's happening, and I don't believe in divine providence. I'd like to do something that's relevant, something else than being a student or a patient. Here it's always analysis and understanding. I can't imagine what your life is like. I suspect you need more drama. I know I do."

"I'm not going to stop you – I don't set the goals – but are you finally talking bluntly and realistically about real and potential disappointment?"

"Are you a Doctor of Disappointment? What good will that do? Should I walk about Harvard Square with placards on my back – a kind of doomsday proclamation of my newly discovered realism and disappointment?"

"Not unless you're looking for converts."

"Are you joking about my unhappiness?"

"I'm sorry if it seemed so; forgive me if it did. A drive for self-expression and seeking an audience has something to say for it; so does a sense of humor."

"My humor is one thing, yours another. Still, you're better than my father's shrink. When Father was talking about his situation at work once, his psychiatrist leaned over and asked, 'What stock is that?' At least you always listen. But I don't pay you, my parents do, and there are times when I would like to do something for you."

"Are you concerned that my needs might become confused with yours, that I might ask something of you?"

"I wish you would."

*

"Have you thought about where else we might live?" Helena asked after Henry had seen his last patient for the day.

"Are you sure you want that?"

Helena was too piqued and frustrated to answer, which Henry misinterpreted to mean that she was not so keen to move after all.

Anyone who gardens believes he has a future. Avalon planted some annuals and brought home a teak bench that he placed at the edge of the lawn in back of the house. That afternoon Prendergast planted a ten-inch-high rhododendron to replace the one he had recently planted beside the entrance to his driveway, which had not survived long in such an unfavorable location. A new twenty-dollar plastic bench, the price tag and bar code still on it, rested uneasily in its new location behind the house, one leg in a crack in the asphalt, another failing to reach the ground.

"He's quiet tonight," Henry said that evening when they had got into bed.

Helena resented his optimism – it hadn't helped so far – and was miffed by Henry's refusal to think seriously about moving, and did not reply.

On the first day of the future, the next morning, the

car was scratched again and the new garden bench had been gouged with an awl or an ice pick. The carcass of another animal, this one too decomposed to make out if it was cat or raccoon, lay carefully placed on the mat in front of their door.

"How can you tolerate this," Helena pleaded with Henry, "not to mention someone wandering about the property at night with a weapon in his hand?"

"I'll call Tim White."

When Henry left for the hospital, Helena called Dr. Boseman, a psychiatrist she had consulted briefly the year before.

14

Avalon brought Timothy White up to date with the details of Prendergast's latest provocations.

"Should we call the police?"

"The problem with calling the police," said White, "is that you haven't got the kind of evidence you'd need. Even a sympathetic judge and jury couldn't do much."

"Could we take out an injunction against him?"

"You could, and he could take out one against you."

"And he could lie."

"There are no consequences for lying to the police, and Lord knows it happens under oath in court. What's legal, for some, is whatever you can get away with."

Henry informed Helena of what White had told him. Desperate, she called the police anyway.

When officer Williams came to the house he was shown the car, the bench, and the carcass. He sat on the new garden bench to fill out his report – the first guest to sit on it, and the only person so far to enjoy it.

"Are you a foreign citizen," he asked Helena, recognizing an accent.

"Yes."

"Sometimes you can get the FBI interested when foreign nationals are involved. I can go over and talk to your neighbor and let him know what the consequences could be if he ever got caught."

"Would you? We'd appreciate that very much," said Helena.

"I don't think he'll be easily persuaded to change," said Henry, "not even by you, but I suppose it's worth a try."

"I hope this is not too discouraging," said Officer Williams. "but something like this happened to me. I put one of the boys in my neighborhood in jail, where he belongs. Now his friends regularly damage my car. There's nothing I can do unless I catch it on tape, or someone who sees him doing it is willing to testify."

"That is pretty discouraging," said Helena.

"Guys like your neighbor are sometimes in it for control."

"That's what they say about sexual abusers. When he calls Henry "faggot", what do you think he's trying to control?"

"He already controls the mood you're in, and whether or not you sleep at night."

Henry's eyes followed Officer Williams as he went next door. "I never expected that a policeman would be more of a kindred spirit than one of my colleagues."

"What he said makes me think all the more that we need to move."

*

"You listened to that nut?" Prendergast kept his gaze directly in front of him without looking Officer Williams in the eye. His view took in the boots and the gun.

"You probably ought to know," said Williams, "in case what he says is true . . ."

"He's a liar!"

"I haven't told you what he said. If what he says is even half-true, you could get into a lot of trouble."

"It isn't . . . I ask because there's no knowing how far someone that malicious is prepared to go with his lies: what kind of trouble?"

"They'd put you in the can."

When Officer Williams left, Prendergast's hand trembled as he closed the door behind him. Later that afternoon he enrolled as a Deputy Sheriff, an honorary civilian position bought with a contribution. He was given a "Deputy Sheriff" decal and placed it in the side window of his car so that if the police came again and saw it, they would be inclined to treat him sympathetically as one of their own.

The gouging of the new garden bench was not the only damage done that night. Before re-entering his house, Prendergast scratched Avalon's car, then his own. Twenty minutes later, standing on his balcony, he whistled as he had before, the same shrill, loud, penetrating, angry sound that had no melody or rhythm in it.

In the morning Prendergast called the police. When Officer Williams arrived, Prendergast showed him the recent damage to his own car, including a scratch directly below the deputy sheriff's decal. It was all dutifully written up in an incident report, including Prendergast's assertion that Avalon had been harassing him for some time and was no doubt responsible for this incident as well.

"What is it?" Helena asked Officer Williams as he

returned to his car, which he had parked in front of her house. He seemed less responsive this time.

"His car's been damaged too," said Williams, "and he's saying you did it."

"Then it's his word against ours," said Helena, abandoning all hope.

"Always was."

"They'll be as ready to believe that we've done these awful things as that he's done them."

"Not necessarily. It's something we've seen before, where the person who's accused pretends the same thing's been done to him. It's called providing your own alibi."

"It sounds as though you believe us, but that there's nothing you can do."

"You could hire a private detective."

"He does these things sporadically. There's no knowing how long we'd have to keep a detective waiting out there."

"They're expensive. You could run a camera."

"We've tried that. You have to reset the camera regularly, all day every day and every night. Even then, you make mistakes, forget to turn on the camera."

"Why don't I give your names to the Cambridge Mediation Bureau? You never know. Once he has to talk about it, it may be harder for things to go on the way they have."

*

"You won't get away with what you're doing to me!"

Prendergast had left his supper on the table and

come outside in the dark where he stood on the top step just outside his kitchen door, shouting over the fence.

"*I'm* doing to *you?*" said Avalon.

"That smarmy remark is an example of how you refuse to talk reasonably with me."

"It's hard to believe that even you think you're being reasonable."

"Don't talk to him," Helena said to Henry, standing behind him just inside the rear door to their house. "Any interaction with him only makes it worse. He has no intention of letting it get better."

Henry ignored her, unable not to respond to Prendergast's provocations. "You mean I refuse to accept your insults and accusations however distorted they are, and didn't construct a fence a hundred feet long entirely at my expense as quickly as you would have liked and entirely according to your whims regardless of cost. Whenever I asked you to put up your share as you were supposed to, or even to say how much you would contribute, I never got an answer."

"Because you're a vile, disgusting person!"

"You've heard of projection, I suppose?"

"That old psychoanalytic jargon. It's had its day; it's through!" Prendergast drew his finger across his throat.

"Then take your meds. Or get some sort of help so that you don't keep doing what you're doing to us."

"Come inside," said Helena. "You shouldn't have said those things to him. Don't talk to him anymore. He's going to punish us now."

"He punishes us whether we say something or not. He evidently feels entitled to that."

"Faggot!" Prendergast shouted from the other side

of the fence and slammed his kitchen door.

"Whatever's wrong with him, building him a fence evidently didn't cure it."

"You've said it yourself: character will prevail."

*

Helena gave birth that weekend to Freddie, a seven-and-a-half-pound baby boy who rode in the car in the new baby seat that had been waiting for him above the wheel whose tire had been slashed and replaced.

"We could record his crying," said Avalon, "and play it out the window for an hour every time the creep wakes us up."

"You're not going to drag Freddie into this, not even on tape."

"If the creep's not a sound sleeper, he won't have much choice."

"It's another reason to move."

15

Prendergast experienced no hesitation or doubt about his ability to carry out the task ahead as he passed through the glass doorway of the Big Brother Agency. That he might not be perfectly suited to the role, or ought to reflect on the motives for his sudden interest, did not occur to him. A nagging shadow of a thought haunted him, not fully conscious, that Avalon had acquired a virtuous patina and that his standing as a citizen had been enhanced as a result of his having a son. Prendergast would not allow himself to be left at a disadvantage; that would be unfair. Envy, he was convinced, did not enter into it. Confident that his motives were sufficiently virtuous, he proceeded unburdened by inner conflict.

Mrs. Molson at the Big Brother Agency smiled sincerely, pleased by the prospect of another big brother. Prendergast's smile was awkward and off-putting, which did not inhibit him from using it. No one had ever called him on it, but then people seldom challenge a smile or question its sincerity. He assumed that it would have the desired effect. And Mrs. Molson was not one to base her opinion, much less a decision, on such fragmentary, uncertain evidence.

Dr. Prendergast, she decided, with the optimism and

charitable disposition responsible for her choice of occupation, might simply be an awkward man. The best way she could think of for dealing with her own unease and his grimace was to smile back.

"He's seventeen," she said. "Is that all right?"

"Why shouldn't it be?" said Prendergast. "I have no prejudices."

"It is so good to hear you say that. I'm sure that Angelo – that's his name – is fortunate to have found someone as tolerant and well established as yourself. We always hope for such good outcomes."

"Are there any legal obligations or liabilities?"

"It's not actually a legal adoption."

"That's what I thought."

"Nevertheless, you will enjoy a special status for him psychologically. This is so particularly when the big brother is an older, mature man like yourself; he's more likely then to become a father figure. The children are told they can call him father if they want to, if he agrees. If you wish to call him your son, we would of course have no objection. In fact, we mention it as an option. It might be nice for him."

"And for me, as well. There are no risks . . . I mean, complications, in such matters as inheritance, and the like."

"None. We do expect you to spend at least half a day with him each week."

"That won't be a problem. I'm grateful to you for giving me the opportunity."

"We like to do what little we can," said Mrs. Molson.

"We're kindred spirits."

Angelo's seventeen year-old black hair matched the sheen and color of his three-quarter length leather jacket. He wore it open, but walked without a swagger, a sign of a precocious maturity in his control of the impression he made on others. He looked older than he was, as if he had worn his mustache for years. Prendergast scrutinized him thoroughly, longer than would have been tolerated in the neighborhoods where Angelo had grown up.

"You must already know all sorts of things," said Prendergast as they walked out of the building.

"I learn what I can, sir."

"Tell me the truth – I'm a doctor – do you take anything?"

Angelo smiled.

"I see."

"Where do you live?"

"Mattapan."

"By yourself?"

"With cousins."

"First cousins?"

"I'm not sure."

"You won't mind a bit of work now and then, will you, in exchange for what I give you?"

"I guess so. What are you going to give me?"

Prendergast thought it premature to answer that. They arranged to meet at Prendergast's house later in the week.

*

Prendergast was still flushed with a feeling of accomplishment at having acquired Angelo when, an hour later in the middle of the afternoon, he received one of his few private patients, Mrs. Jennifer Marston, in his living room.

The dark wooden mission chair she sat in was too large for her and insufficiently upholstered to provide much support; left to her own devices, Mrs. Marston could not summon the will to straighten her back. Prendergast found her despondency hard to tolerate. He was not inclined to pity, except in principle. Confronted with a person who might provoke it, he quickly sought relief, the favorite form of which was a passionate righteousness and the statements and actions it inspired.

"You have to act!" he said to Mrs. Marston. "You need to do something for yourself for a change."

"I'll try," she said, pulling herself together and squelching her tears and, as much as possible, her feelings with them. She talked haltingly about her sixteen-year-old son, Johnny, recently discharged from the psychiatric clinic where he had been hospitalized for truancy, drug abuse and a propensity for self-endangering behavior. He had been re-admitted to the clinic when she and her husband had stopped talking to each other.

"You've told me that before." It was her second appointment with Prendergast. "Are you and your husband still living together?"

"We've been separated for a while now, though we're still under the same roof."

"You hadn't told me that. How do you manage it?"

"He lives on the top floor of the house in a separate apartment, and we, that is Johnny and I, live on the floor below."

"Mrs. Marston, I want you to think of what you can do for yourself. The next time we meet you'll tell me what that is."

"*I'm* supposed to tell *you*?"

"I'm not averse to telling you myself, but I would first urge you to come up with a plan of your own."

"What shall I do meanwhile with Johnny?"

"Let's see how he does now when he's out of the hospital . . ."

"They refused to keep him. They said he wasn't going to kill himself, or anyone else, so they discharged him."

" . . . and how he adjusts to what you're going to do to take care of yourself – when you've figured out what that'll be." Prendergast rose from his chair.

"Is that all?" Mrs. Marston had been in the office fifteen minutes.

"There's no point letting a session drag on . . ."he added, "if nothing important's happening. French psychiatrists – they're ahead of us in this – will ask a patient to leave as soon as they feel enough has been said, even if the patient's been there only five minutes."

"Do you mean if he doesn't say what the doctor wants to hear, he banishes them?"

Fearing her question was too aggressive, she backpedaled.

"It can take a while to get to what you need to say."

"As in anything else, you can train yourself to be quicker and more efficient. The clear focus and tight structure I'm providing will help."

She kept her slouch when she stood up, and had a headache now on top of her exhaustion. She felt uncertain on her feet as she walked out of Prendergast's house.

71

16

"Were going to mediate," Avalon said to Waring over lunch.

"You never know; it could be useful." Waring's willingness to be encouraging, however, went only so far.

"Has your neighbor been like this with anyone else that you know?"

"You're not the only one who will find it difficult to believe what's been happening." Avalon's pain at having to defend the truth of his story was visible, though Waring seemed not to notice it. "He looks good on paper. People will think that someone with his credentials just doesn't do such things. I've had trouble believing it myself. Every time something happens I try to think of who else could have done it until I finally have to accept that he's doing it, deliberately."

"Be careful at mediation."

"They'll be well-meaning, at least, and want to help."

"I don't want to be pessimistic, but if they're do-gooders, you may be in trouble. The PC police are everywhere. Your neighbor sounds like the sort who's good at persuading himself, and others, that *he's* the victim. He'll have the advantage if he can sound more aggrieved than you."

*

The Neighborhood Mediation Service was located in the Senior Citizens' Center and met in a small conference room that served a variety of other functions as well. It was furnished with a file cabinet and bare walls.

"Lord knows if this is worth it," said Helena as they rode the elevator.

"We need to do this, if for no other reason than to keep Officer Williams' good will," said Avalon. "It won't help if they think we're unwilling to give it a try."

Prendergast wore a pale suit, a thin tie, and the fake alligator cowboy boots that had everything but the teeth in them that he had worn to the singles' event where he met Priscilla. They went largely unnoticed and out of sight while he sat at the table. His smile, fixed and prolonged, was an imperfect fabrication. Combined with his eyes, which he kept wide open so as not to lower his brow in a scowl, it brought him close, in Avalon's imagination, to an imitation of a saint at the moment of receiving the holy spirit, or the axe that would have martyred him in a piece of late medieval art.

The Avalons, unable to arrange a babysitter, had brought Freddie with them. The mediators, two earnest social workers, no doubt had good intentions. One smiled, the other didn't. The one who didn't, spoke.

"We're here to provide a venue outside the courts

for parties to negotiate solutions to their differences. What is said here, as the form you're asked to sign indicates, is confidential and cannot be used in court, except in criminal cases."

Prendergast maneuvered quickly. "I would like to say how grateful I am for the opportunity you've provided us."

Both mediators smiled. Together with Prendergast they looked at the Avalons to see what they would say. Neither Henry nor Helena felt particularly grateful for the opportunity of being there, and it probably showed.

"Officer Williams," said Avalon, "suggested we give this a try."

That sufficed for the moment.

"Why don't you admit it," said Prendergast. "You hate me, don't you?"

Henry and Helena, stunned by the abrupt confrontation, did not answer. Prendergast went on.

"The problem with Mr. and Mrs. Avalon . . ."

"Is that to be the starting point, that we're the problem?" said Henry.

"Actually," Prendergast smiled in Helena's direction, "I have no problem with you."

"Everything you've done to Henry you've also done to me." Helena pulled further away from him. "Henry and I are together in this."

"Oughtn't we all try to behave here, at least?" said Henry.

"What do you mean?" Prendergast turned to the mediators: "I don't understand his innuendo. I hope that, as mediators, you won't be influenced by it; I was just being polite, and precise, in what I said to Mrs. Avalon."

"Is that why you're here, to be polite to my wife?" Henry turned to the mediators. "It was an obvious, if clumsy attempt to manipulate her. Perhaps we ought to talk about why we're here."

That said, the mediators turned their gaze back to Prendergast.

"When these people built an addition to their house, without any warning or consultation with me . . ."

"I'm sorry to interrupt," said Henry, "but we've been over this point. I showed him the drawings before we began, once in his house, and once in ours."

"I noticed when we were in your house that you had a hunting scene on the wall. Do you engage in blood sports?"

"Only when I try to deal with you. In any case, you acknowledge that you saw the drawings."

"Do you know that he thinks global warming is a good thing? He's completely indifferent to the consequences if the winters in his corner of the world can be a little warmer."

"You are?" asked the formerly smiling mediator, her face too earnest for a smile to survive.

"It was a joke. Dr. Prendergast's joke – not a very funny one – is to pretend that it wasn't."

"The Avalons promised to build a fence between our properties. They have fallen woefully short of their obligation."

The mediators turned to Avalon.

"What he's left out – he invariably fails to mention something important – is that the Zoning Board decided we were both to contribute to the cost of a new fence. When I got the bids from various fence companies and tried to talk with him about what we would each contribute, he never responded. The result is that he got an unnecessary_new fence, which he was supposed to help pay for, entirely at our expense. What he's complaining about, and the reason why he's been vandalizing the fence we built for him, is that it isn't exactly the kind of fence he wanted, which would have been illegally high without a special permit, and the most expensive fence conceivable."

The mediators turned to Prendergast, but it was Helena who spoke.

"He does, however, communicate with us. He deliberately wakes us up nearly every night; he has several times scratched and dented our car and punctured the tires – directly under the baby seat; he's thrown rocks at the fence between our properties and pulled it apart in places so that it looks disheveled like his own property, leaving the broken parts in our driveway; he has placed dead animals in front of our door, shouted insults, calling my husband faggot and taunting me with sexually harassing signs that he hangs in his windows, defaced the other fence in front of our house along the sidewalk, and roamed our property at night with an ice pick in his hand gouging the garden bench. Lord knows what's next."

"Similar things have been done to my car." One had to know Prendergast to tell that the feeling with which he spoke was false. "I have the receipts from the garage that made the repairs. Perhaps someone else in the neighborhood has done these things to both of us."

"You'll find that his receipt has a recent date on it, after we called the police to tell them what's been happening. The harassment we've experienced has been going on for months. After the police came to tell him to stop hounding us, he damaged his own car to make it look as if he was a victim too."

Prendergast held out his hand so that the mediators could see it shaking with the feelings that were was through him,.

"These are sly and menacing people. I feel seriously menaced. I am constantly in fear living next to them. My adopted son, Angelo, who grew up with tremendous privations, was terrified recently because of the way they dealt with him."

"Do we have to put up with this humbug?" Avalon asked the mediators. Helena stepped on his foot under the table to remind him to control himself. "Isn't it transparent what he's doing? Incidentally, if you check the records you'll find that he hasn't adopted anyone. It's a program they have at the Big Brother Agency which he signed up for after our child was born. The incident he's mentioned was when the boy was playing music so loudly that several neighbors called the police."

"We must be even handed," said the mediator who didn't smile.

"Negotiation takes time," said the one who did. "We may need more time for this, more meetings."

"I would appreciate that," Prendergast smiled.

The atmosphere of the meeting, being in such close proximity to adults with strained expression and tone of voice, was disturbing to Freddie. He had cried on and off and wouldn't stop now as he filled his diaper.

"I'm sorry; there was so much going on when we left the house, I forgot to bring an extra diaper," said Helena. "I didn't expect to be here this long."

"I'm willing to stay the rest of the afternoon if it will help," said Prendergast.

"I have to leave," said Helena.

"We may not have had a chance to talk enough," replied the mediator. She managed a faint replica of her former smile.

"It would help if there were some recognition of what we're up against," said Avalon.

"Wouldn't you all benefit if you kept talking?"

"Recently," said Prendergast, following her suggestion, "I found rags covered with paint and turpentine in the alley on the other side of my house."

"We know nothing about them," said Helena, alarmed, and looking at the mediators with a new intensity. "If he's suggesting that we might start a fire, it's something we have never spoken of or even thought about, though, as you just heard, Dr. Prendergast has. The rags he speaks of were probably left by the men who were recently doing some work on that side of his house."

"I want to underscore what my wife has said," Henry added, "to you, and to Dr. Prendergast. He's sometimes confused about who is doing what to whom."

"I'll admit I could have acted better at times," said Prendergast. "I may have thrown a few pebbles at the fence once. I'm a man of feeling. Should I be blamed, given their provocations? They haven't acknowledged anything of what they've done to me."

"Dr. Prendergast is inviting us to join him in a *folie à deux*," said Avalon. "He began here by asking us to admit that we hate him. I doubt that anyone in our position could like him after what he's done, but that's beside the point. Dr. Prendergast may have identified the right feeling, but he attributes it to the wrong person. He's confused about who's feeling what about whom, which makes it hard for a third party to know what's going on, or whom to believe. Even when you're faced with something like this yourself, it's hard to believe that it's actually happening."

"You have to admit that you've been giving me the window treatment," Prendergast said, glaring at Avalon.

"The window treatment?"

"His window shades are pulled down nearly all the way, except for an inch at the bottom."

"So?"

"Do you deny that you're doing that to make me nervous; are you suggesting that you're not spying on me?"

Henry and Helena looked at the mediators. Not knowing what to say, they thought they would at least look professional if they maintained a serious, neutral expression and said as little as possible.

"If the positions of our window shades had anything to do with you," said Avalon, "they would be pulled all the way down to screen you out, not to provoke you or spy on you, which would only stir up more trouble. Can't you believe that the window shades might be in their positions for other reasons than to have an effect on you, that we're not thinking of you all the time, that the positions of the shades are random?"

"He wants us to admit to things so that he won't look so bad for what he's done," said Helena. "We haven't done anything to him."

"Liar!"

Prendergast was so loud and spoke with such intensity that everyone was silent, until he spoke again.

"I'm teaching a course at the Bunker Hill Community Clinic on narcissism. Perhaps you would like to come and listen."

"We don't have to go that far to learn about narcissism from him," said Helena.

"That paper we signed," said Avalon, "said that mediation isn't intended to deal with criminal matters. The behavior we're talking about is either criminal or warrants psychiatric treatment, both of which lie outside the purview of these meetings, however well intentioned they are. Another problem is that mediation implies a possible justification for his behaviors – which can't be justified."

"We need to go," said Helena, doing her best with Freddie.

"Mediation takes time," said the mediator who smiled now perhaps because the meeting was over. "Before you leave, shall we schedule another meeting?"

"I would be glad to do that," said Prendergast.

Henry hesitated.

"Perhaps, but let us think about it."

"Why should we do it?" whispered Helena as they left the conference room.

"So that we don't look as though we're the ones who are unwilling to talk," Henry whispered back.

"If you want a relationship with me," said Prendergast, "If you want a relationship with me . . .?

"I don't want a relationship with you," said Helena. "I want a divorce . . . from you, not you, Henry, though I'm beginning to think that you can get rid of a husband more easily than a neighbor. What do you want from us? You demanded a new fence and you've got it, but you still send all sorts of things over it so that one way or another you are always in our space; you can't stand us but you imitate us and want to keep talking to us. Won't you please leave us alone?"

Responding to the intensity in his mother's voice, Freddie fortunately began to cry again and the Avalons left.

"Henry, his malevolence surrounds us; it's with us all the time. Others hear about one fragment or another; the menace that's relentless and always with us isn't evident to them. I don't think I can live with this."

Henry had no better answer than the mediators had offered; not knowing what to say, he was silent. When his anger had subsided enough, he shivered.

"The meeting with the mediators hardly seemed real. Our dilemma is real."

He felt a disaster being born and saw no way to stop it.

"No one wants to make room in their thoughts for horror; they don't want to hear about it; they want nothing to do with it – except in a movie."

*

Prendergast lingered with the mediators after Henry and Helena left.

"I'm entirely in favor of what you're trying to do," he said.

The smiling mediator said "Thank you;" the other nodded and said nothing.

"I can't speak for them, of course."

"I'm afraid you can't," said the one who didn't smile.

"We'll have a chance to hear from them the next meeting," said the one who did, as her colleague left the room.

"I agree, we ought to meet again. Meanwhile, perhaps you and I could meet."

"I don't think that's quite the way it's supposed to be."

". . . so that you could tell me more about how this works."

"Oh, I see."

"Then you will?"

"I don't know."

"Strictly a professional consultation, some evening, this evening, perhaps."

"Perhaps an afternoon coffee."

"It's still afternoon."

*

After bathing and changing Freddie at home, the Avalons, needing some pampering themselves, went to a local restaurant and afterwards, walked home.

"Look! It's Prendergast?" said Helena as they approached the house.

"With another woman, not the one we saw before."

"It's one of the mediators!"

They stopped to watch from a distance.

"He's trying to persuade her to go inside with him."

"She seems to have refused."

"Barely . . . this time."

*

Prendergast fetched himself a drink and settled into the same mission chair where Mrs. Marston had sat in his living-room.

The glow of the television was not warm enough to dispel the atmosphere he had created for himself at home. Unaware of what compelled him to go out, he went to a nearby college cinema showing a documentary about sharks. Inside the theatre, he nodded to Dr. Lee, a sometime colleague at Middlesex County Hospital, whose sense of his own authority, in serving as a judge of his peers on the state Licensing Board for Mental Health Professionals, left his face emptied of expression.

The narrator of the film, a voice familiar from television documentaries on the natural sciences, informed the audience, as a great white shark clamped its jaws onto a young seal, that "while at first sight this may seem cruel, mother nature insists that life must fight to survive. After millions of years, predators have become better at killing; but at the same time, their prey has become better at defending itself so that only the strongest predators and prey continue to thrive." As the seal's blood spread into the water around the shark, the narrator continued: "In any given encounter, however, one or the other must prevail."

Among the sea of distraught faces in the darkened theatre, Prendergast's face was uniquely impassive. Lee nodded in agreement with the narrator.

*

In his sleep that night Prendergast dreamt of his experience more than thirty years ago at the Army Draft Board; he had been called up the summer before entering medical school. He behaved as badly as he could, doing everything he could think of to make himself insufferable. Yet when the doctor issuing the exemption from military service said, "We don't want you either, Prendergast," he felt rejected and angry. On his way out, he took a calendar off the wall.

*

Dr. Lee remembered no more dreams that night than he did most nights, that is, none at all. He doubted that he dreamt much. It was only because researchers had declared in scientific journals that everybody invariably dreams several times a night as part of the sleep cycle that he grudgingly allowed he might now and then have had a dream without knowing about it. He had reservations about the argument that dreams had meaning, and an attitude verging on contempt for theories assuming the existence of the unconscious; he was devout in his belief that the future of psychiatry needed to be developed on a strictly empirical, unencumbered by theory. Yet he privately had made room in his mind for philosophy of another kind, his nightly ritual based on an Ancient Asian philosophy. When he returned home from the cinema he threw his *I Ching* sticks on the table and consulted the ancient text:

Biting through has success. It is favorable to let justice be administered. The theme of this hexagram is a criminal lawsuit . . . When an obstacle to union arises, energetic biting through brings success . . . Deliberate obstruction does not vanish of its own accord. Judgment and punishment are required to deter or obviate it.

Dr. Lee nodded his approval and went to bed.

*

The next morning on Adams Street, the Avalons saw that the roof of their car had been struck and dented in several places by an awl wielded with considerable force.

"I only have to see the car now to be reminded of what's going on."

"We've been talking of buying a new one; there's no point in doing that now."

"I'm not sure we should go ahead with plans to fix up the house," said Helena. "He may spoil whatever we do."

"That way we'll never do anything and our house will eventually look like his."

"Despite the fence he draws us into his world."

The Avalons went ahead and repaved the driveway in red brick, constructed a latticed framework for roses across the height and length of the porch, and scheduled a painter for the fall.

"They use invisible electric fences to keep dogs in," said Avalon. "Shall we see if they'll keep him out?"

They agreed to see about it, but forgot to. It was too much out of character, too far from the way they were naturally inclined to operate, to contrive so many schemes and maneuvers to defend themselves. They simply didn't want to live that way. But they were not so indulgent with each other. On the occasions when

Prendergast renewed his campaign of harassment, their failure to follow through with various technological deterrents became a cause for mutual reproaches.

They looked at ads listing houses for sale, but everything they saw fell short of what they already had. They ran a camera again at night, irregularly. On the nights when Prendergast did further damage they had invariably forgot to turn it on. Then there were mutual reproaches for the lapse in vigilance, and unspoken anxieties about the consequences of their bickering.

"Let's not allow this to ruin things for us."

"Yes, let's not let that happen."

*

"I don't know that I can take it much longer," Helena said the next day in Dr. Boseman's office. Initially put off by his basement office and by the frustration of her wish that he do more for her, she had got used to him, and his basement.

The way Dr. Boseman gripped his pipe in his teeth lent emphasis and authority to what he said.

"Henry is still unwilling to move?" he asked.

"As much as ever."

"And you've tried to talk with him about it?"

"Repeatedly."

"Do you think he has to be in control at all costs?" This was hardly the sort of neutral comment his training years ago would have recommended. He found it hard not to respond to Helena's appearance of vulnerability and helplessness; it enhanced her beauty for him as she described the difficulties on Adams Street.

"Maybe," she said, opening her mind to the idea for

the first time and rapidly becoming angry. "I suppose he doesn't have to agree with me," she added in an attempt to control her anger. Uncertainty as to Henry's motives might be safer in the long run.

"Nor you with him."

"Are you saying that it would be a mistake if I did? In any case, I doubt he's going to listen."

"Is there something we haven't taken into account? Do you think he's uncomfortable with the prospect of your graduating and obtaining qualifications that will enable you to be independent?"

"I hadn't thought of that. Maybe."

*

Henry's review of the situation with Prendergast over lunch elicited from Waring: "You still resent him, don't you?"

"He hasn't given me much opportunity to stop resenting him. I suppose it's hard for you, for anyone to believe that a member of the profession will do things like that."

Waring was inclined, for business and other reasons, to align himself among his acquaintances according to the prevailing winds and shifts in power and prestige, despite his frequent criticisms of those on top. It was a "matter of survival." Judging by what he had heard of late from Cobb and others, Waring suspected that Avalon's star, so recently rising, had already passed its zenith, and saw no reason, none consistent with his goal of survival, to go to any pains to maintain the friendship. Unsympathetic remarks came easily. He would not have denied that friendship has inherent value, if one has the time for it, but he was a busy man.

*

"Tell me now, Jennifer, what have you done for yourself since I last saw you?" asked Prendergast the next time Mrs. Marston came to his office. He liked to address his patients by their first names; he thought it consistent with seeing patients in his living room.

"I've been thinking . . ."

"In other words, you've done nothing."

"I was thinking of Johnny. He's under so much stress – it's been hard for him for so long now – my moving out might be too much for him."

"You're not thinking of yourself, Jennifer. It would set a good example for Johnny if you were to let him see that you can take care of yourself. You seem to know what you have to do."

Mrs. Marston looked at Prendergast from behind her splayed hands, as if they were guarding her face, while he wrote her a prescription.

"Perhaps you won't feel so bad about it when you've taken this."

17

The voice on the answering machine, neither gruff nor menacing, was too practiced to sound friendly. The message was from Cobb, informing Avalon that the group that had met to talk about literature was disbanding for the rest of the year as he had said it might at their last meeting. However, if Avalon were interested, Jane Bruckner organized speakers for talks by psychiatrists on various topics; he might want to contact her.

The accumulated memories of numerous micro-perceptions had left Avalon with the impression that he would not fare well if he approached Bruckner, whatever the occasion. It was not without misgivings that he called to ask if he could be of any help.

"No," she said. Not "Let me think about it" or "Not at the moment" or "I'll get back to you"; not even "No thank you," just "No." Like Cobb, she had not forgiven Avalon for saying more than she had at the recent meeting of the group with literary interests.

Avalon tried to fill the silence with some follow up, saying "Good night." It fetched no reply.

18

On their walk the following weekend Henry and Helena heard a rustling sound in the woods on the hill above them.

"I heard that sound in the woods again."

"So did I."

"I didn't just hear it. I think I saw someone running."

"What was it?"

"You won't believe it; it's too strange."

"Are you going to tell me?"

"I could swear it was human flesh."

"That's not so peculiar – could be a jogger without a shirt."

"If it was a jogger he was completely naked, except for a touch of color in his mid-region."

"A pair of shorts."

"Too small for that."

Mendelson was running naked through the woods again. True to his principles – in this case the one that had recently inspired him to speak about the central importance of ambivalence in every relationship – one testicle was green, the other red. All he was wearing was a touch of make-up; he had used face paint to color one testicle green, the other one red. Whatever the object of his ambivalence, it did little to inhibit him that afternoon. The recent signs of his career's advancement had put him in an expansive mood not easily contained.

*

A package addressed to Prendergast was delivered by mistake to Avalon's house. On the shipping label Avalon could see that it contained a book entitled : *How to Succeed In Local Politics.*

"He would never be elected," said Helena. "He can barely get a date."

"He doesn't look that off-putting if one doesn't look too carefully. In politics he wouldn't have to stay close to anyone long enough for that."

"If he ever did get into office, I have no doubt that he would do everything he could to use his position to make us miserable if we continued to live here."

"Let's not be pessimistic. We'll deal with that if and when it happens."

Henry scribbled a note on the package requesting the postman to redeliver it to the correct address.

19

It was one of their blessings that, in spite of everything, vacation came again for the Avalons as it had in other years. They went to the place by the sea where they had always gone. Their worries evaporated in the shimmering white light that flickered on the water and suffused the air. The landscape seemed more inviting than at home. Being away reassured them that escape was possible and that for a while, at least, they had accomplished it.

During the last fortnight the Avalons were away, Prendergast began alterations to his house without consulting the Zoning Board or obtaining a permit. From time to time he occupied himself with cementing his relationship with Angelo.

When the Avalons returned, Prendergast said to Angelo:

"I'm going away for a week. I'd like you to look after some things for me while I'm gone."

Angelo did not have to ask what was in it for him. He understood perfectly well that Prendergast expected something from him in exchange for goods and services rendered, and that he was already in Prendergast's debt. Not one to leave things to chance when pursuing his passions, Prendergast thought it prudent to reinforce the bond.

"I imagine you'll find this useful." He handed Angelo a blank sheet from a prescription pad.

*

The day before he left for his own vacation Prendergast found the largely decomposed carcass of a squirrel infested with maggots in the park across the street. He picked it up carefully with a shovel, in case the squirrel had been rabid, and placed it on the mat in front of the door to Avalon's house. It was lying there when he and Helena returned.

"His welcome home," said Helena.

They called the police, as they did regularly now when an incident occurred.

"It's all so demoralizing." Helena looked miserable and felt too despondent to be angry.

"It gets to me too," said Henry.

"We'll run the cameras."

"We never catch him. We're not going to set the alarm and wake up half way through the night every night to change the tape. When we have caught him on tape it's never been anything more than a hand, or the top of his head, nothing we could use as evidence. In any case, he usually manages to do something on a night when we've forgotten to turn on the camera. We would have to be as obsessed and relentless as he is in order to catch him."

"Who's pessimistic now?" said Helena. They divided the emotional work between them, changing places as bearers of hope and despair.

"Look what he's done to his house!"

Various balconies, railings and other features inspired by nostalgic notions of architecture had sprouted on the outside of Prendergast's house, regardless of the effect on its overall design.

"He lacks a sense of design," said Henry, "as others lack a sense of hearing or smell."

They did not know where Prendergast had gone, or for how long, but took some comfort in his being away. For four nights the Avalons' kept their camera running. On the fifth night they forgot.

*

During that night, and two more nights in the following week while Prendergast was away, the Avalons' car was damaged. "Prendergast is a cautious man," said Henry. "He's reckoned that one alibi might not be enough."

"Henry!" said Helena, waking him up one morning after having fast-forwarded through several uneventful hours recorded by the camera. "There's someone on the tape. He's walking by our car where it was scratched."

Looking in the camera as he played the tape, Henry saw Angelo, with his black hair and raincoat, walking onto their driveway and taking something out of a small black bag slung over his shoulder as he came alongside the car.

"We've got him."

"But it's not Prendergast!"

"Whoever he is, I saw him once going into Prendergast's house."

"There would only be your word for that. I doubt it

would connect him to Prendergast in court."

"He must have some connection to him."

"So do people who have never been in our driveway. And you may be the only one who's ever seen him going into Prendergast's house."

"Why would he do this for Prendergast?"

"Drugs? Money? Prendergast might have given him prescriptions in exchange for services rendered."

"Wouldn't he be risking his license?"

"Maybe not, if the prescriptions were just within the limit of what one's allowed to prescribe. Allegations about his motives wouldn't amount to much in court either."

"I still think that if he's the boy I've seen going into the creep's house, we ought to go to court."

"How do we stop him from doing further damage?"

"I'll put a sign on the car at night: 'Dear young man, whoever, you are; we've seen you and caught you on camera. Don't put yourself at risk for the creep next door."

"That may protect the car from him; it may also frighten off a potential witness whose name we don't have yet."

"It's more important to persuade him not come around again."

Helena placed a sign on the car. From then on Angelo was no longer photographed by their camera.

The incident was duly reported. The reports to the police accomplished nothing more than accumulating a paper trail in the hope that if the volume of such incidents were large enough, it would, if the matter ever came to court, be harder to dismiss their complaint as having no merit. Meanwhile, unable to live with the prospect that the current situation with Prendergast might continue indefinitely, they contacted their lawyer, Timothy White.

"We could go to court," said White. "If he were convicted he would be in serious trouble. But Henry's right. Even if you proved that the kid in the film has ties to your neighbor, that by itself doesn't prove that your neighbor got him to do it. *I* believe you, but I'm not the one you have to convince. You'll need more than you've got to get a conviction. But we can try."

*

The Avalons and Timothy White reviewed their evidence in preparation for their appearance in court: the pictures of the defaced and damaged fences, the damaged car, the dead animals, the knife left in front of the door, the gouged bench, receipts for repaired tires and body work on the car, various shots on tape showing a hand or the back of a head as one act of vandalism or another was being perpetrated. Each item, despite their resolve to keep their hopes in check, roused feelings of excitement at the prospect of finally putting an end to the long period of mayhem and harassment, not to mention the nights of disturbed sleep, excitement that was followed by doubts about how they would fare in court.

"I suppose there's nothing we can introduce as evidence to show that he wakes us up two hundred nights a year."

"No, there isn't."

"Or the fear instilled by his sinister, nocturnal whistle – I felt my pulse shoot up the other day when I heard a passer-by whistling downtown."

"Nor that either."

"They may think the evidence we have is not tied to him convincingly enough."

"They may."

"Couldn't they, with a sufficiently thorough examination, determine that the top of the head in one picture, or the hand in another, is his?"

"That would be unusual."

"The courts prefer precedent."

"Exactly."

20

Outside the courthouse, Prendergast ran into Christopher Lessing, SJ, MD, a colleague and a priest.

"I hope you're not in trouble," said Prendergast, unwittingly revealing, in the hope that Lessing was not in difficulty, a fantasy that he might be.

"Not for the moment."

"I hope you don't mind, I can't help being curious why you're here."

"I'm here as a spectator."

"I didn't know you cared," said Prendergast, assuming for a moment that Lessing was there as a sympathetic spectator at his trial.

"Cared? How do you mean?"

"Oh . . . I had a particular case in mind, that's all."

"If you're curious to know why I'm here, I come to watch trials as Victor Hugo attended public hangings. It's a personal interest of mine in matters – in my case legal matters – I don't know much about, but that I'm trying to understand."

"It's been a while since we were residents together; I wonder if you could be of some help in a case I'm involved in."

"It has been a long time. I'm afraid I don't see how I could be; I don't know anything about the case."

Dr. Lessing's jacket slipped back just far enough for Prendergast to catch sight of a gun in its holster.

"You carry a gun, you . . . a psychiatrist, and a priest!" This turned Dr. Lessing, in Prendergast's view, into the perfect witness.

"Sorry, it's not for hire."

"Why do you carry it?"

"I occasionally visit some very dangerous places. Mostly I like the way it feels. We have feelings too, you know, even eccentric ones. Sorry I can't be more help."

"Thank you for your *interest.*" Prendergast could not suppress a note of sarcasm. It had no apparent effect.

*

As a final compromise in the protracted struggle between the architect and those who controlled the state purse, the courthouse had cost too much and looked ill-fitted, unfinished and disheveled from the day it opened.

"The old courtrooms," thought Avalon, "the kind you see in the movies, had solid features worth looking at." He had always liked the old wooden chairs with their curved armrests, the wooden balustrades separating the spectators from those involved in the trial, the slow turning fans overhead, the replicas of Roman railings in the windows. There was nothing to look at in the new courthouse. The courtroom had no windows. The fake wooden veneer on the walls looked thin and cheap in the gleam of fluorescent lights. It was a setting for styrofoam cups, for concentrated boredom and anxiety.

Events unfolded in court precisely as, in his most

pessimistic moments, Timothy White had feared.

"So far," said the judge, who found their progress tedious, "I've heard nothing but charges and counter-charges."

"If you please, Your Honor," Timothy White replied, "we should like to show the court two video tapes of Dr. Prendergast committing acts of vandalism and harassment."

"Real evidence! By all means."

The first tape showed Prendergast inserting an eight foot long, three-inch wide, rusty brown iron pipe into the ground along the fence near the door to Avalon's office – precisely where his patients could not fail to notice it – then cover it with oil so that it would be difficult to remove. Because the camera had been placed in a window where it looked down from above, and because of Prendergast's position directly underneath, one saw the top of his head with its bald spot, the tops of his hands and the shoulders of his jacket, but not his face. One did not see much more of him when, after finishing the job with the pole, he pulled a plank out of the fence that ran between the two properties in the same vicinity, so that a person on Avalon's side of the fence would have a full length view of the pole.

The second tape showed the same man, again photographed from above, this time wearing a tweed cap, using a spray can to deface the fence in front of Avalon's house along the sidewalk.

"I can't see the face," said the judge.

"Who else could it be, Your Honor, in either of these scenes?"

"'*Who else*' is not a strong legal argument."

"If you look at the plan of the properties, Your Honor, you'll see that the business with the pole and the destruction of that part of the fence took place at their rear. To think it could be someone else is tantamount to believing that someone other than Dr. Prendergast (1) trespassed on Dr. Prendergast's property, (2) carried a large iron pole thirty yards or so onto Dr. Prendergast's property to that particular part of it, and (3) for no gain to himself spent twenty minutes there erecting a the pole and greasing it, then some more time pulling a plank out of the fence."

"I can't imagine anyone I know doing anything like that, but how does what you've shown prove that Dr. Prendergast did it?"

"Your Honor, with modern technology we could probably enhance the image and get a good enough picture for an expert witness to match it with the features of Dr. Prendergast's hands and head, proving that he is indeed the person in those videotapes."

"I don't know of any precedent for that. In making your suggestion you don't even specify which kind of expert testimony the court should seek; it's hard to imagine who would do it. Your request is denied."

"Your Honor," White appealed to the judge on other grounds, "it is finally up to the court whether Dr. Prendergast will be allowed to continue his career of harassing the Avalons and maliciously destroying their property."

"Objection," said Prendergast's lawyer. "He speaks as if it were established that Dr. Prendergast is involved in any of this."

"Objection sustained. I must remind you," the judge said to White, "that I shall decide what the court will do."

"You once told me that I don't know who's doing what to whom," said Prendergast. "How do you come to be so sure that you know any better? My property's been damaged too."

"The defendant will address the court," said the judge, "and not speak directly to the plaintiff."

"Nearly everything that Dr. Prendergast belatedly alleged to have happened to him," Timothy White said to the judge, "happened considerably earlier to my clients, and over an extended period of time."

"It looks as though someone has been vandalizing a number of people in the neighborhood," said Prendergast's lawyer.

"Only one party has, for a long time, been repeatedly vandalized," said Timothy White, "by Dr. Prendergast and one of his hirelings."

"Objection."

"Sustained."

"What Dr. Prendergast claims was done to him," Timothy White persisted, "happened much later, after months of his harassment of my clients, and then only after they called the police. Your Honor, the police themselves have told my client that people who harass others in this way will try to provide an alibi for themselves, when the need arises, by doing similar damage to their own property."

"Objection. It's nice that the police in his neighborhood chat with the residents, and maybe not so nice that they take sides," said Prendergast's lawyer, "but counsel for Dr. and Mrs. Avalon has not demonstrated that that has anything to do with my client."

"I'm afraid he has a point," said the judge. "Objection sustained."

"I would respectfully submit, Your Honor," Timothy White replied, "that conventional police wisdom and police knowledge in such matters should carry some weight."

"Isn't knowledge a wonderful thing?"

"Your Honor," Timothy White continued, in an attempt to sidestep the sarcasm of Prendergast's lawyer, "as the video tapes we presented may not have been sufficient, we would like to present the court with further evidence, including an audio tape taken from Dr. Avalon's telephone answering machine, letters and other communications between Dr. Prendergast and my client."

The court heard Prendergast on the audiotape say in a gruff, resentful voice: "You haven't responded to the letter I sent you three days ago asking when you would start construction on the new fence between our properties. I'm not going to be pushed around, or let you get away with not answering . . . Faggot!" The words were followed by some vulgar sounds.

"That's very odd," said the judge, "very odd. Nevertheless, as you know, it's protected by the First Amendment."

"As Your Honor will have noticed, the defendant is so coercive in his behavior with my clients it never occurs to him that the reason they have not got back to him might be because he himself has been so offensive or, as in this incident, because my clients were out of town. Your Honor, what you just heard was followed a day later by this letter in which Dr. Prendergast tells my clients, assuming he had the right to address them in this way . . ."

"He has the right, counsel, but what did he say?"

"He orders my clients to 'begin construction of a fence between our properties ten feet high of flat planks topped by another two feet of lattice. The construction of the fence will begin by the end of this month. I shall inspect the fence as it is constructed on a daily basis so that any requests I may have for changes can be complied with. Should the construction of the fence continue beyond two weeks I shall deduct one hundred dollars from my contribution to the cost of the fence for each day completion is delayed.'"

"Evidently Dr. Prendergast agreed to contribute to the cost of the fence."

"One would think so from that one sentence in that letter, and Dr. Prendergast did in fact agree to contribute to the costs of a new fence at a meeting of the city zoning board. But repeated efforts by my clients to ask him precisely what he would contribute were ignored, as were the estimates from three different fence companies that my clients secured and sent copies of to Dr. Prendergast. The only thing my clients could count on was that Dr. Prendergast would imperiously and abusively make demands of them."

"What did your clients, or Dr. Prendergast, do next?"

"My clients sent Dr. Prendergast a letter making the points just mentioned, in reply to which Dr. Prendergast sent my client the following letter."

Timothy White showed the judge a letter illustrated with a smiley-face tab, subscribed underneath with the words: "Suck cheese, shark face."

"That's very odd, very odd, I admit."

"And offensive, Your Honor."

"It is conceivable that a person may have been

offended, but none of this constitutes evidence that Dr. Prendergast committed the various criminal acts you say he has."

"It does, Your Honor, reveal something of the character of Dr. Prendergast, and that should make it more plausible than ever that the actions perpetrated against my clients, actions that are unusual, even bizarre in some instances, could be done by the sort of person that wrote such a letter."

"'Plausible,' again, is not a strong legal argument. And Dr. Prendergast's name is not even signed at the bottom of this letter as it was on his previous letters."

"It uses the same font as Dr. Prendergast's previous letters, one not available to the Avalons; and who else . . ."

"I've told you that 'Who else?' is an argument that has no legal weight."

"An examination of the machine this was printed on would certainly . . ."

"Do you want to go to that extent over the matter of a fence?"

"It's not so much a fence, but relentless harassment, malicious destruction of property, and disturbances of the peace responsible for hundreds of nights of lost sleep. Dr. Prendergast repeatedly imposes outrageous demands on my clients, and intrudes himself into their lives. He sends a variety of things – obscene language, pieces of the existing fence he has destroyed, dead animals, and himself, ice pick in hand – over the fence onto my clients' property, the same fence he bullied them into building after having misled them about his willingness to make a contribution to its cost, the same fence he now deliberately damages and tries to dismantle. In similarly confused and confusing behavior, even as he persists in such hostile behavior with Dr. and Mrs. Avalon, he also imitates them."

"Imitates them?"

"When my clients acquired a bench, Dr. Prendergast acquired a bench; when Dr. Avalon shaved his beard, Dr. Prendergast shaved his beard; when my client had a child, Dr. Prendergast 'adopted' one, so to speak."

"So to speak?"

"It's not actually a legal adoption . . ."

"Not a legal adoption?"

"It was done under the auspices of the city's Big Brother program."

"I see . . ." Turning to Prendergast, he asked, "Why did you shave your beard?"

"I like to be honest, and I decided that beards hide things . . ."

"So do trousers, not to mention lying and deceit," said Avalon.

"Dr. Avalon, you will speak only to the court."

"I prefer to be an open book," said Prendergast.

"Your Honor, anyone can hear the humbug in what he says."

"The court hears what Dr. Prendergast says, but has no way of ascertaining whether or not it is humbug, which is not a legal term. What he said was in the proper format, at least, unlike your outburst just now.

"Clearly," the judge instructed the jury, "damage has been done to Dr. and Mrs. Avalon's property. And it is entirely possible that the harassment they say they have suffered occurred precisely as they say it did. Even so. . ."

". . . *even so*," Helena whispered to Henry. "We've lost."

". . . you must decide if these things were done by Dr. Prendergast. The only one we know definitely to have done any of these things is the young man you have seen on the videotape, and we know that one of the incidents in question occurred when Dr. Prendergast was out of town. We know there is a connection between that boy and Dr. Prendergast, who volunteered to be a Big Brother to the boy. The story the prosecution introduced about the boy's being suborned by offers of drugs, however, is merely an allegation. Their argument to the effect that 'who else' but Dr. Prendergast could have done so much over the extended period of time in question may not be entirely without merit, but does not constitute evidence. Nor do the videotapes allegedly of his head and hand. The officer's remarks about how some youth in his neighborhood did something similar to him, and that perpetrators of criminal harassment are apt to do something similar to their own property to provide themselves an alibi, are also not relevant to this case for lack of sufficient evidence, and therefore not to be taken into account in considering Dr. Prendergast's guilt or innocence. Like everything else he is alleged to have done, it is certainly possible, you may think plausible, or even likely, but you must decide if it is proven. That *they* have seen him – while no one else has – of course does not matter at all and can not be considered as evidence."

"That's that," said Helena.

Timothy White, also foreseeing the outcome, kept his head low, avoiding contact with Henry and Helena. They noticed this; interpreting it correctly, they lowered their heads as well.

*

After his acquittal, Prendergast, who long ago had been at college with the judge, tried to say hello to him. The judge, possessed of a surer sense of decorum, or of self-preservation, than Prendergast, slipped out of the courtroom before Prendergast could reach him.

"If there's any truth to those allegations," he said to the court clerk, "Prendergast ought to consult one of his colleagues for some professional advice."

Angelo, who had been a co-defendant in the trial, was convicted of malicious destruction of property, handcuffed in the courtroom and escorted by a guard to a holding cell in the courthouse basement.

"One of you is finally put away," said Officer Williams as Angelo passed him on the way downstairs.

"Why do you say that?"

"Someone like you did the same thing to my car too."

"He did it to *you?* Did he know you were a policeman?"

"You heard the story in court. I sent another like you away. Afterwards his friends in the neighborhood went after my car."

"You're a cop. Why didn't you get him?"

"Couldn't, not without catching him on film, as they did with you."

The lesson that what had befallen the Avalons could also happen to a policeman abruptly changed Angelo's ideas about his future career. From time to time he had imagined it would be prudent to become a policeman, an idea he had clung to even while awaiting trial, and had not been inclined to relinquish until this moment.

He expected eventually to elude the consequences of his sentence one way or another, perhaps by moving to another state or befriending a policeman as he had befriended Dr. Prendergast. But other ways to power and success now captivated his imagination: Dr. Prendergast seemed to lead a charmed life, and the lawyers, he noticed, were better dressed than anybody else in court.

*

Reminding himself that he was a man of conscience, Prendergast went downstairs for a word with Angelo.

"You have to get me out!" Angelo pleaded. More than ever now Prendergast seemed to Angelo skilled and powerful, particularly in what was required to get the best of his enemies and keep himself out of trouble.

"I would if I could," said Prendergast in an avuncular, low-pitched voice. "Unfortunately they got their hands on evidence that's incontrovertible."

"It was you who put me up to it."

"That's not the same as doing it. There are all kinds of considerations in a matter like this. I admire you for not talking, but if you had, I would have had to deny it. If you want to be strong, you have to realize that you're the one responsible for your own actions. As it's a first offense . . ."

His pride prompted Angelo to correct him: "It was the first time I got caught."

"As it's the first time you've been caught you, the sentence will be a light one and you'll come out wiser at the end of it."

"You mean I should have been more careful?"

"Exactly."

*

Mr. Lementov and Mr. Reilly, one a functionary of the Democratic party in the city, the other similarly employed by the local Republican organization, came to the courthouse in nearly identical, dark gray, ill-fitting suits. Within minutes of each other they asked the guard on duty at the information desk the same question: "Where can I find Dr. Prendergast?"

The guard looked through the list of employees.

"He doesn't work here."

"I know . . ." said Reilly.

"He had a trial here today," said Lementov before Reilly could say the same thing.

"What's he accused of?"

"Acquitted. He may be an important man one day. He may still be in the building. Can you tell us where he is?"

The guard shrugged. "Knowing that's not part of my job."

Just then they caught sight of Prendergast as he returned to the ground floor lobby after his conference with Angelo.

Lementov and Reilly looked at each other, then Lementov said, "I believe we've come to tell you something similar."

"Perhaps," said Reilly.

"Are you going to tell me what that is?"

"I represent the Republican Party in Cambridge, Dr. Prendergast, and my colleague . ."

"The Democratic Party," Lementov interrupted, reckoning he ought to be the one to identify himself. "You wrote to us a while back."

"And to us. We liked the style of your letter."

"As did we. You wrote to Repubicans and Democrats?"

It was good, after the trial, to hear others suggest that he had something to look forward to. Sudden advances in politics, even for those without much background in them, were not unknown. "It probably isn't appropriate to talk with both of you at the same time. Shall we arrange to meet separately to see what can be worked out?"

*

Despite his victory in court, Prendergast took no notice of the clear light and strong colors of a late summer day except for the painful effect on his squinting eyes of the sunlight reflected off the pavement. He felt oppressed by the prospect of the ongoing tribulations of living next door to the Avalons, and was as angry as ever that the new fence in the style he had stipulated had not yet been built. The ever-larger holes in the deteriorating old fence in front of his house along the sidewalk did not bother him.

He remembered, and again was stung by Avalon's taunt: "Then take your pills," when he had dismissed psychotherapy with the contempt it deserved. He had remained unsure whether Avalon had been hurt by the insult he had laid on him about psychotherapy's obsolescence, but until now no fitting retribution had yet come to mind. Now, out of his suffering, finally came a plan pregnant with the promise of justice and reparation. It would take some doing, but he was, he reminded himself, more clever and resolute than Avalon, and would ultimately prevail. As the idea that now captured Prendergast's imagination unfolded he glowed at the prospect of satisfying a fundamental desire; it stimulated and refreshed him, and made him indifferent to the humid heat.

Not for years had he felt so elated and exultant as he did in that moment when the idea for a final solution to his problems with Avalon came to him. Nor in all those years had he concentrated on any piece of work as he did on the letter to Avalon he carefully drafted when he returned home.

Dear Dr. Avalon,

I could nurse my grievances about the recent trouble and expense I was put to at the trial, and there are colleagues who would think it untherapeutic to deny my feelings about the injustice of its having taken place at all. But that would be backward looking. What's more, although your scheme failed in court, that does not mean that everything you say is wrong. You once told me that I had problems of a psychological nature and suggested, if I interpret correctly what you said in the heat of an argument, that I ought to seek treatment – in particular, psychotherapy – to help me deal with them. I know this will seem bizarre to you, unbelievable perhaps, but I would like to try a period of work with you as my therapist or, as I prefer to think of it, my consultant. This would be on an experimental basis. You'll understand that it will be hard for me to trust you completely after what has happened. Nevertheless, I've been impressed by your tenacity, and by the fact that while your style is so different from mine, you nevertheless appear to have succeeded in life, your recent effort in court excepted of course.

Yours sincerely,
Albert Prendergast

"In principle, it would be the perfect solution," he thought. "It may be hard for him to believe that I would actually present myself to him as a patient. It has to be believable." Prendergast remembered the exchange with Helena when she said she wasn't Mrs. Avalon and he said he wasn't Dr. Prendergast; the feeling of excitement and anticipation returned. He wrote a second letter.

Dear Dr. Avalon:

I could nurse my grievances about recent trouble and expense I've been put to. It may be a better alternative however, to have some therapy, though I am a practical man, and prefer action to talk. For reasons of precaution, and because I require an unusual degree of privacy and discretion, I would suggest, if you agree to take me on for some consultations, that we undertake to work by phone. This would be on an experimental basis, of course. You will understand that it will take time for me to trust you more fully. If you are willing, please call. The number of my cell phone is 1-617-508-

113

1221. Should you agree to my proposal, I would of course call you for the appointments. With guarded optimism, I look forward to our joint effort.

Henry showed the letter to Helena.

"It's too bizarre."

"I've treated others who were scarcely more revealing. If someone is a bit paranoid, but knows enough to know he needs help . . ."

She cut him off, afraid he might talk himself into it.

"This is a trap. There are other therapists in town. He can go to one of them."

"Well, exactly. That's what I'll tell him." Avalon phoned Prendergast and left a message:

Thank you very much for your interest in working with me. I appreciate your request, but given our history, I believe it may be better for you to work with someone else. Please let me know if you want a referral.

Prendergast did not take this lying down. It was important to reply quickly to Avalon's latest insult, and to avoid giving any hint of having taken offence.

Dear Dr. Avalon:

Thank you for you thoughtful reply. It demonstrates qualities I value. I appreciate that my proposal is, of course, unusual. On the other hand, it presents a possibility of treatment for me, and no obvious danger to either of us. I have not given up, and look forward to your coming around to my point of view. Think of what a remarkable case it would be if the treatment were successful. As for payment, you could tell me each week or month what I owe and I would send you a check.

"Don't do it!" said Helena when Henry told her about the second letter. "Rescue fantasies are an occupational hazard. If he ever showed up, I wouldn't be surprised if he came wearing a disguise."

Prendergast was late for the first appointment, missing half of it. He rang off half way through the second for reasons he refused to talk about. They agreed on the fee during the third appointment. The fourth was missed without prior notice.

The occasion Prendergast was waiting for came with the monthly bill. According to the custom of the profession, he was charged for the missed appointment.

"It's the custom in the profession, as you know, to pay for sessions that are missed without twenty-four-hour notice," said Avalon when Prendergast told him that he was so offended by the charge that he was not going to pay any portion of the bill.

"And I disagree with it."

"Have you thought of the position you put me in when you don't show up and don't pay?"

"A position where you're not paid for work you haven't done."

"And left with an hour that I could have spent earning my living if I had known you wouldn't call. It's not like a dentist's or a general practitioner's office; they schedule so many in a day there's always someone in the waiting room ready to come in."

"Who was the therapy for, you or me? I find it hard to talk to you, and you haven't helped me with that. I've said more to you in letters than I've been able to say on the phone. We ought to admit that the treatment's a failure."

"If you insist. But do you really mean that you don't see there's an issue here in the way you deal with another person? Perhaps it's easier to talk about the smaller things: you know that if a person's late it could mean that he's angry."

"And if he's early he's anxious, and if he's on time he's obsessive. Are you in it just for the money, or to tell me what's wrong with me? Too bad you were left with time on your hands, but I'm not obliged to pay for it."

"Very well, if you wish to bring things to an end.. ."

"If it's going to end now, you'll have say it's over; I won't. It doesn't surprise me that you want to push a patient out, regardless of his need."

So it ended; so Avalon thought.

"It's over," said Avalon after giving Helena a brief case history.

"I wouldn't be so sure. He may not have come in and he may not have paid, but bad relationships don't necessarily depend on payment or frequency of contact. You may never be able to get rid of him. I warned you."

"Your warnings made me think it would be far worse."

"It may be yet."

*

The next day when the Avalons were out, at Prendergast's request, the McClaren Tree and Landscape Company came to Adams Street. Certain trees that grew on the Avalons' land spread gracefully over both sides of the property line. After the arborists left, boughs that had provided shade on Prendergast's side were reduced to stumps protruding an unsightly foot or so from their trunks.

21

Arthur Winfield had just given one of his public lectures which he delivered each year in partial fulfillment of his obligations as University Professor of Moral Values – a lecture Angelo attended in partial fulfillment of a parole requirement that he seek further education to help him become a better citizen. The lecture had been about the Triumph of the Church Therapeutic. The lecture hall was not far from Adams Street. Prendergast was also there, curious to see if there were other arguments against psychotherapy in addition to those he already had – or that it should be divorced from medicine altogether and returned to clergymen.

After the lecture Prendergast went up to Professor Winfield and introduced himself.

"You bring up some interesting ideas."

"Thank you, thank you." Winfield's honeyed, mellifluous voice, soothing to listen to, sweet and rich in tone, lent a gracious quality to anything he said.

"Do you think there's a need for a new politics as well?"

"It sounds as though you have some interesting ideas yourself."

"Difficulty in gaining access to power and influence

is one of the principal problems that we face now."

"That is an interesting idea. Very interesting."

"I would imagine there are any number among those you and I know – even you and I – who would do a better job in political office than those who are there now."

"No doubt, no doubt."

"No one at the university has yet, for example, thought of setting up, under university auspices, a special unit with vans to patrol the town in order to enforce the values that are so important, yet are openly flouted."

"I don't know about the enforcement part. That could be complicated."

"The basic idea is that both Left and Right are so cynical, so empty when it comes to values . . . Politics have become little more than horse trading, politicians striking deals. There is no concern any more about being right."

"Being right . . . that can be complicated too."

"Or any interest in stopping those who are wrong, even saying that they're wrong. Would you have time for a walk? I could try out some of my ideas with you, about a new platform, and possibly running for office, as part of a sustained campaign to turn these ideas into something real."

"It would certainly be interesting to talk about it some more but, if you'll excuse me, not today. It may sound old fashioned, but I still believe that work ought to be put aside on Sundays."

"Henry Avalon! It's been a while."

He recognized Avalon from his time as visiting chaplain to the to the Belair Hospital.

Henry and Helena, who were out for a walk, were passing in front of the hall where Prendergast held Winfield captive. Prendergast knew when to withdraw.

"Do you know him?" asked Avalon.

"I was just beginning to."

"Be careful. You may want to steer clear."

"Thanks for the warning, though I must say I agree with some of the things he said, *some* of them. He seemed a bit eccentric, but who doesn't?"

Avalon didn't argue. It was, he reckoned, the same problem he had faced elsewhere; there was no way to convince anyone about the nature of Prendergast's character who hadn't directly experienced it. If he tried, the chances were that Winfield wouldn't believe him, or that some of what made Prendergast so off-putting would rub off onto anyone describing it.

23

There wasn't a cloud in the sky on the day Mendelson secured his promotion to full professor at the Medical School on the basis of his work on Affect Deficiency Syndrome as a new psychiatric diagnosis. Feeling exalted and free of conflict, and unable to contain himself, he ran up and down the wooded hillside behind his house at the time of day when Henry and Helena Avalon took their walk.

"For a while now you've carried a pair of binoculars on our walks," said Henry.

"You have too – sometimes."

"I know. I wonder if we should bother to take them."

"There's always a chance of sighting an exotic bird. I confess, I've been hoping that we'd get another glimpse of whoever's been running through the woods."

"That's more exotic than any bird."

"I wasn't sure you were interested, or I would have explained it earlier."

"I heard a twig break."

"Sh-h."

Mendelson ran by twenty yards above them, too elated to look down the hillside where the Avalons stood silently, largely camouflaged by trees and undergrowth that were thick enough to leave them unsure of precisely what they saw.

"I thought I saw some color, too," said Helena, "but everything here is green."

"He was stark naked."

"Could you make out who it was?"

"For a moment I thought I did, but . . . it's all too strange. I doubt it."

*

When they arrived home, Henry found a letter from the State Licensing Board for Mental Health Professionals, signed by Dr. Lee.

As if he were examining a patient, he recorded his own reactions – bated breath, difficulty focusing his attention as the world dropped away at his feet and he slowly grasped that he was at the edge of a cliff.

"What is it?" asked Helena. "The creep? You look as though you're afraid of him again."

"It's not helpful to tell me I'm afraid. Aren't you? In any case, this is something new."

He held out the letter for her to read:

Dr. Avalon:

Please reply to this complaint by your former patient, Dr. Albert Prendergast, within thirty days of the date of this notice. You may retain legal counsel if you wish.

For The Board, &c.

"You have nothing to worry about. You've done nothing wrong."

"I've heard these Boards see themselves as advocates for the consumer."

"So?"

"The consumer is always right. They're political appointees, not necessarily the most sophisticated clinicians. They can rationalize whatever they do by saying that they're protecting patients and the profession."

"There would have to be some evidence that the patient's been harmed."

"Evidence is a term from the courts. There have been struggles for hundreds of years to determine what can be allowed in evidence in a court. This may be a trial, but it won't be in a court."

"It was hard enough to get the court to consider the little evidence we had, and they didn't finally. I don't see how he could possibly be in a stronger position than we were. Don't worry; it's not becoming." She reached up to put a tuft of hair back in place.

"That's not helpful either."

"I'm sorry, darling. I don't want to be difficult, but I can't help thinking it's another reason why we ought to move."

"The licensing board has state-wide jurisdiction."

"To another state, then. I wouldn't mind a better climate. There's no point sticking around here waiting for global warming. . . . You hesitate. Are you afraid of moving, too?"

"It would be a lot to give up, though for a moment, I confess, I felt relieved to think we might escape."

"You had better prepare for this; you'll need Timothy White again."

What Avalon could not put into words was the feeling that all that he had built over several years with hard work, which had recently been coming to fruition, was slowly exploding and he could do nothing to stop it. One usually can't with explosions, even slow ones. He had expected to progress naturally to the next stage in his development; instead, he had encountered Prendergast, who was for all practical purposes a parasitic life form dedicated to his ruin.

*

That afternoon a photographer from the local newspaper stood outside Avalon's house taking photographs of his patient, Geoffrey Parsons, walking back and forth along the pavement with placards on his back and chest reading: "If the end is at hand, will therapy help?" The day before, the placard in front of him had read "Hope", the one in back "Despair"; the day before that, "Excitement" and "Lost Desire".

A police officer stopped and leaned out the window of his cruiser to question Parsons.

"Why are you demonstrating?".

"I heard a lecture by a Dr. Mendelson on the inevitability, the all pervasiveness, the profound universal truth of ambivalence and its relation to Gefühlsarmut."

"What?"

"Affect Deficiency Syndrome."

"Whatever. But why are you demonstrating here?"

"My therapist's office is here."

"Is that a message to him" – he pointed to the placards – "or the general public?"

"I'm trying to give expression to my confusion and frustration."

"Yes!" said Prendergast who was walking by on his way home and heard only the part about expressing one's frustrations.

"You would rather do this than take your ideas to him directly?" asked the policeman.

"I've done that. When I told him I might do this, he thought it would be a sign of progress if I did."

"Wearing placards?"

"Expressing myself."

"Wouldn't it also be a sign of progress," said Prendergast "if you went further and fired him as your therapist?"

"Eventually, I suppose, I might move on."

"What you're doing now could be seen as a form of harassment," said the police officer, "particularly when it's going on just outside his door."

"He hasn't objected, in which case, it's a matter of free speech."

Prendergast nodded.

"They say that about everything now." The policeman decided that it wasn't police business and drove off.

Turning to Prendergast, Parsons suddenly recognized him.

"You gave a talk at the Middlesex County Hospital on how the relationship between a psychiatrist and his patient should be a negotiation?"

"I thought it was about clarity of communications and enhancing control. Negotiation is involved in that. You're in treatment with *that* one, aren't you?" Prendergast gestured with his head towards Avalon's house.

"Yes, but it's not enough. We talk, and I do most of the talking. I suppose that's the way it's done."

"Used to be; still is with those who are old fashioned. But there are other ways."

After giving the matter a moment's thought, Parsons said, "I know this is unorthodox, but I think I might like you to be my therapist."

"Then you'll be my patient, but you ought to tell him why you're leaving him first." Prendergast imagined the scene with relish.

"Thanks for the advice," said Parsons, pumping up his resolve. "I will."

The smoke from Prendergast's cigar blew not altogether accidentally in Parsons' direction.

"Whenever I can be of help . . ." said Prendergast, giving Parsons his card. He carried some with him in the event of such emergencies.

*

When Parsons appeared at Avalon's office for their next scheduled appointment, he laid his placards on the floor and placed his skateboard on his lap. This was a new development; he had previously left the skateboard on the floor with the placards.

"Are you about to scoot?"

"I have to talk to you about something."

To signal that he was listening, Avalon tilted his head in a way that gave him the air of a wise man.

"I had an appointment with Dr. Prendergast."

It wasn't hard to intuit what was coming.

"He said that I was empty and had serious characterological problems, that I had to do more to deal with my situation."

Avalon crossed his legs, but they didn't stay long where he put them.

"I'm going to be seeing him, instead of you."

"If you think that's best. I'm sorry this has happened, that you're caught between two doctors."

"He said I had to tell you how I felt about you first."

"Your feelings about me are always a legitimate topic and welcome. Perhaps you feel put on the spot when you've been asked to talk about your feelings for your therapist as a requirement for being treated by someone else; that would encourage you to talk about only negative feelings."

When Parsons did not reply, Avalon asked: "What is it?"

Parsons burst into tears.

"He must have made quite an impression."

"He promised that he would be able to *do* something."

"And that seemed more attractive than sitting still and finding out what's going on inside you."

"I'll stay . . . but shouldn't our relationship include more negotiation? Isn't there more that I can *do?*"

"It's an interesting idea, maybe a good one, as long as it doesn't come to resemble something that might transpire between two lawyers. How useful it would be would depend on what was being negotiated and how it was done."

"You often make things complicated."

"It's sometimes part of my job."

"I wish there were more that I do . . . for myself . . . and for you."'

*

What Prendergast saw as Jennifer Marston's obstinacy, she felt as a fear that pulled her shoulders down and made it hard to talk.

"Jennifer," Prendergast said to Mrs. Marston, "you've supposedly been separated from your husband for seven years, while living under the same roof with him. The situation is confused and static. It's stuck and can't evolve into anything new. In order to de-confuse it you will have to do something: either get back together with your husband, or leave him."

"Could that be a problem for Johnny? He's so unsteady now; his condition seems so precarious. I don't want to make it more difficult for him than it already is."

"We've talked about that. What good do you think you're doing for him by tolerating the current situation indefinitely? Do you want him to grow up to be a man who puts up with any situation in which he finds himself, who is unable to make decisions or to impose his will on others and his environment? For his sake, as well as yours, you may want to think of putting an end to this arrangement that has gone on for so long and that, for all you know, has contributed to Johnny's problems."

"Do you think it's done that?" she cried out in alarm. The pain cut very deep.

24

In a state of sympathetic and enraged excitement Dr. Jonathan Lee watched on a television screen that dominated the living room wall, a program about the time of the Red Guards in China. File footage of the Cultural Revolution showed Red Guards and villagers "struggling", as they put it, with a teacher, a dentist, a scholar, a farmer, and others whose occupations or attitudes were regarded as historically regressive.

"We would surround them and tell them what was wrong with them," said a middle-aged, former Red Guard, *"tell them the crimes they had committed against the people. Sometimes we would shout at them, sometimes hit them."*

"Did you like hitting them?" asked the interviewer.

A stirring in his entire being caused Dr. Lee involuntarily to sit up straight as he heard the Red Guard's answer.

"At the time, yes. We became addicted to hitting people and pushing them around. We looked forward to it. We felt virtuous."

*

"I think about it all the time," said Henry, but there's not much we can do."

Helena would have preferred to tell him once again that they ought to move, but with Henry already feeling helpless she feared that would only fetch an irritable reaction.

"You could ask Mendelson to help out."

"We've never had that sort of friendship. I'm not sure he's the type . . ."

"He may be a little manic and eccentric, but he isn't nasty, is he?"

"I suppose a little mania doesn't hurt anyone, but . . ."

When Henry failed to give more of an answer Helena offered the only thought that came to mind.

"Darling, why don't you see the soothsayer?"

"Again?"

"It's a particularly difficult time . . . you never know." Seeing his reluctance, she added: "Do it to humor me. By the way, Mother is coming from Greece for a visit."

"Will she be staying with us?"

"No, with a friend of hers in Boston. She speaks French, Italian, some German, but not much English. I'll need to spend some time with her."

Avalon winced.

"What is it?" asked Helena.

"It hadn't occurred to me until I just felt it. I won't relish being at home alone with the creep next door. It won't even feel like being at home."

"Oh, Henry! It's not just my mother and I who are foreigners here. The creep makes you a foreigner too, in your own home."

*

The fortune-teller drew the window curtain to close off the view from the street. She wore the same long dress of brightly colored Indian cotton and a kerchief on her head.

"You're back," she said, "in spite of your skepticism." As a sign of her growing prosperity she had re-dyed and styled her hair. The couch had been reupholstered in a fabric that matched the new curtains. The price had changed too.

"That will be ninety dollars; no checks."

Henry was tempted to say, "You mean, 'no taxes.'"

After looking in her crystal and examining the palm of his hand, she said, "You will have trouble with a neighbor."

"You're more accurate this time, but you're timing's off."

"How is that?"

"I've been having trouble with a neighbor for some time."

"Do you have reason to think the future with your neighbor will be any different from what it's been in the past?"

Avalon was surprised to hear her say something that sounded insightful and true. It robbed him of the derision and contempt with which he had been prepared to dismiss whatever she said.

*

The day before the hearing at the State Licensing Board for Mental Health Professionals, Avalon went to see Dr. Koestler, his former analyst.

"It must be serious to bring you back," Koestler greeted him.

Avalon told Koestler what had been happening with Prendergast, bringing him up to the latest chapter – his own imminent appearance before the State Licensing Board for Mental Health Professionals.

"He's tried and failed to get what he wanted in mediation, and he barely held his own in court," said Avalon. "I'd like to think he won't be more effective with the Board."

"It was you who took the case to court; he wasn't there to accomplish any goal of his. His purpose in mediation may not have been simply to get a new fence, but to keep the fight going. Most of the time he's pursued that goal outside the formal venues. Now that he's resorting to one voluntarily, I shouldn't underestimate his cunning. That and his implacable hatred make him very dangerous."

"In psychoanalysis, at least, you can take the time you need to get things right. In those other settings supposedly dedicated to sorting out the truth, time runs out before that can be done."

"In psychoanalysis one writes with a pen, in politics and the law, with a fence post. In the short run, the fence post has a stronger impact."

"Dr. Koestler, what do you think of the Affect Deficiency Syndrome?"

"There's a lot of it about suddenly. An extraordinary range of behaviors are being linked to it, in papers that lack scientific rigor in their concept, method and reasoning. They may have taken a valid idea, as they did with high-end autism, and make it ridiculous applying it to everything."

Koestler's dog, Venus, who had been lying on a rug across the room and recognized a familiar face or, more likely, with cataracts on his eyes, a scent from the past, paddled with difficulty across the floor of the office and licked Avalon's face as he lay on the couch, as she had done during the years of his analysis.

"Much as that annoys me," said Avalon, "I can see the difference between that and Prendergast's whistling. When I hear anyone whistle now, I grow tense with fear and anger. I have no particular reaction when I see a dog."

"It's not surprising that love should have a different effect on you than hatred."

The favor Venus had bestowed on Avalon and Dr. Koestler's comment reminded him of Parsons.

"I have a patient, a young man, who wants to do something for me. I don't know how to handle it. You and I talked once about how difficult it can be to be spontaneous and appropriate."

"It's tricky – for the patient and for the psychiatrist."

As Avalon got up to leave, Koestler left him with, "I know he's hard to ignore, but your neighbor is too much on your mind. You need to think of Freddie and Helena. There is only so much of this she'll be able to bear."

At one o'clock in the morning Prendergast whistled his monotonous, loud, shrill, angry whistle, waking Henry and Helena.

*

Moments after Mrs. Marston arrived for her

appointment with Prendergast, he said to her, "You haven't told your husband yet, have you, Jennifer?"

"You can tell?"

"Isn't that why you look sheepish?"

She nodded.

"Come back to see me when you've told him." Prendergast stood up.

"You mean I have to leave now? Isn't it early?" The appointment had barely begun.

"I'm afraid so. There's no reason for sessions to run the same length every time, regardless of whether anything worthwhile is going on."

Before leaving she turned to say: "Please be gentle with Johnny if you see him again, Dr. Prendergast. The one time he saw you, you ended that session sooner than he expected. He had the impression that you would see him only so long as he said and did what you wanted, and that, if he didn't, you had no interest in working with him and would throw him out."

"My technique has a purpose. It provides therapeutic leverage for modifying behavior. Johnny is a boy with many problems, Jennifer, some of them no doubt inherited. He's told me about your family and its history."

"I know I never told you much about them. You never asked, and I wasn't sure you were interested in that kind of information. I think I tried once but you were concerned then about bringing his behavior under control. Dr. Prendergast, this has all been so devastating. It was once a distinguished family."

"According to Johnny, his father is a bastard, and the same was true of his grandfather and great grandfather."

134

"Johnny isn't looking good these days, Dr. Prendergast. I'm worried about him." She wrung her helpless hands.

"Let me know when you're ready to see me again."

25

Avalon and White made their way across the gray, barren concrete moonscape of government buildings in downtown Boston.

"You've done some preparation," observed Timothy White. "You carry your briefcase as though it were full of lead."

"I've been doing nothing else, and I still don't feel prepared. I don't know what to prepare for."

"They don't tell you much."

"They are colleagues. You would think they would want to be helpful."

"This Board in particular has been pretty severe. Other lawyers I know who've dealt with them say they're a rogue board. So far this year they haven't let anyone off. The last client of mine who came before them really didn't deserve what he got."

"Do you do much of your work here? If you do, I assume you would need to maintain a working relationship with the board."

"Yes . . . though I would sue them if I thought it appropriate."

"That's very reassuring."

The small hearing room was furnished with standard government furniture: a metal table, three metal chairs behind it for board members, and two in front of it for the psychiatrist defending himself and his lawyer. The walls were bare. Dr. Jonathan Lee entered the hearing room wearing tight black jeans, a roughly ironed white shirt with a youthfully narrow collar, and a black string tie. Henry Avalon and Timothy White wore suits. He shook hands as if it were a real gesture and smiled briefly with just the ends of his mouth. After inviting Avalon and Timothy White to sit down, he remained standing behind the table, looking down at Avalon as he spoke to him.

"You'll have read the complaint. Have you seen patients like Dr. Prendergast before?"

"I'm not sure what you mean. I've been practicing for twenty years, during which I've worked with several persons of his age and profession."

Dr. Lee shifted from his left foot to his right like a dodging boxer waiting to deliver a blow, though his movements were less pronounced. It drew Avalon's attention to his black jeans, which were always moving in front of him at eye level, and the Western string tie that swung to and fro.

Not knowing quite where to begin or what to say – it was not yet clear precisely what the Board or the energetic Dr. Lee wanted from him – Avalon spoke slowly and haltingly. Lee noticed Avalon's discomfort and let it continue a while.

Avalon read an account of the case from his notes. He offered Dr. Lee the results of tests a psychologist had administered, to the extent that Prendergast had allowed it. He let go of the report, assuming that Dr. Lee, who at first seemed ready to take it, had it securely in his hand. But after a quick glance – he could not have seen much, or had caught sight of something he would rather not have seen – Lee withdrew his hand and the report fell to the table. Shifting his weight from one foot to the other he impatiently interrupted Avalon.

"And his diagnosis?"

"I thought I had already said that he was borderline and paranoid."

Lee did not comment on Avalon's diagnostic formulation, effectively brushing it aside.

"I may as well tell you, this is about Gefühlsarmut Syndrome, Affect Deficiency Syndrome, ADS in short."

"This is about Affect Deficiency Syndrome?"

"Did you know that since seeing you Dr. Prendergast was seen at the Belair Hospital where he was diagnosed with Affect Deficiency Syndrome?"

"I don't see how I could have. He evidently went there after he saw me, and no one at the Belair contacted me."

"What do you think about their having given Dr. Prendergast that diagnosis?"

Avalon had no idea how to respond. He sat with his hands on his knees and the empty, placid demeanor of an Egyptian statue. Dr. Lee's rapid-fire interrogation demanded his response and blocked it at the same time. Avalon started to move the paper with the data from Prendergast's psycho-logical testing data that was altogether inconsistent with that diagnosis, back in Dr. Lee's direction. It was hard data, not just another clinician's guess at a diagnosis. Dr. Lee paid no attention to the piece of paper Avalon pushed across the table, keeping his gaze fixed on Avalon.

"Then you would not diagnose Dr. Prendergast with

ADS? You dismiss out of hand the diagnosis given him at the Belair Hospital?" The implication was that an entire medical institution was at odds with Avalon.

"I would be hesitant to accept it automatically. I would want to know what it's based on. I've shown you data that's inconsistent with it. There's a group at The Belair that specializes in patients with that diagnosis and they give it to nearly everyone they see. It's a diagnosis that's suddenly very current, but it's not included yet in the Diagnostic Manual. The new edition isn't out yet – it's in press – and there's already talk of removing it from the next edition."

"One of our members," it was a way of speaking that made the Board sound rather like a private club, "is particularly concerned with Affect Deficiency Syndrome."

"Is this about his concern or about the legitimacy of Dr. Prendergast's diagnosis?"

"Are you being flippant?"

"I don't understand; suddenly this diagnosis is all important."

Timothy White intervened: "We had no way of knowing that this would be the focus of the hearing."

"Admittedly, councilor," Lee addressed White with a degree of respect he withheld from Avalon, "the Pervasive Developmental Disorders are a gray area."

"A gray area?" said Avalon. "You mean that we don't really know what we're talking about. Then why should I be in trouble for having chosen another diagnosis, particularly when it's based on objective test results, and the diagnosis attributed to Dr. Prendergast at Belair comes from a group that has a particular interest in that diagnosis? We all know diagnoses that have come and gone. Pseudo-Neurotic Schizophrenia, for example, and Borderline Schizophrenia, not to mention Neurosis itself, which is not completely gone but seems to be increasingly out of fashion."

"Don't you realize the position you're in?"

Avalon tried again, ignoring Dr. Lee's warning. "There hasn't been a single reliability study that would clarify what Affect Deficiency Syndrome actually is. I know four experts in the field of Pervasive Developmental Disorders who recently met to look at the testing data for a sample of people who might have had it and they couldn't agree on a single one."

In response to the interrogator's silence and Timothy White's puzzlement, Avalon explained, "a reliability study enables you to know that your means for assessing different samples of a thing will reliably tell you they are at least samples of the same thing."

"Are you suggesting that The Board doesn't know what a reliability study is?"

"Mr. White here wanted to know. But everybody ought to be cautious when experts can't agree."

"Are you trying to instruct the Board? I have a touch of ADS myself, and I have no reason to doubt that Dr. Prendergast does too. Mendelson has helped us all to appreciate how widespread it is."

"Is he the one who saw Dr. Prendergast at the Belair and diagnosed him? He's recently made his career writing about Gefühlsarmut Syndrome, which he prefers to call Affect Deficiency Syndrome, and he sees it everywhere . . . Anyway, what is it precisely that I failed to diagnose, if there's so much disagreement and uncertainty about what that particular diagnosis represents? If ADS is supposed to be a Pervasive

Developmental Disorder that afflicts people who can communicate articulately but still have trouble relating, it could apply to almost everyone."

"That's precisely why it's so useful clinically."

"Then even you're saying there isn't anything precise about it. It will be very convenient for the insurance companies, as they say psychotherapy is of limited use for those who are supposed to have it."

"Your problem is compounded by your having offered psychotherapy to someone with ADS when that's not the treatment of choice."

"He came to me for psychotherapy. A person with ADS might still reckon that he's got things to talk about in psychotherapy. To deny that is like denying there's a human life to be lived by anyone with this diagnosis."

Dr. Lee was for a moment a silent, but hardly benign, presence in the small, airless room. The silence kept the pressure on, and though Dr. Lee had jumped on everything he'd said, he tried something else.

"Please look." Avalon held up the psychological testing scores for Dr. Lee to see. "According to this, his understanding of what goes on interpersonally fetches his highest score, and one that's above the national average. If Affect Deficiency Syndrome or ADS leaves a person without feelings and with no understanding of what's happening interpersonally – a kind of autism – then ADS is not his problem, though he may be paranoid and cunning. Prendergast has plenty of feelings – he's overwhelmed by them – and he's all too involved interpersonally. To say that he has ADS is like saying black is white."

Dr. Lee looked no longer at the paper that Avalon held up than he had before when he had let it drop to the table.

"You will acknowledge, won't you, that this," Avalon indicated the testing, "makes a difference?"

Lee didn't answer. He turned to a computer at the end of the table and typed a note.

Avalon whispered to Timothy White: "He's not answering my question."

"Because he has no answer," White whispered back, "and because he doesn't want to, and because he doesn't have to. You want to be quiet, or he'll become angrier. I'm not sure how much this is any longer about that Syndrome or the patient. Whatever else, it's certainly about the authority of The Board and their power, and his anger, and the right they have to punish you."

"It couldn't be as debased a process as that."

"He wouldn't see it that way. He believes they're doing a public service."

"Did you know," said Dr. Lee, "that since Dr. Prendergast went to the Belair Hospital and was diagnosed with ADS, and been prescribed a standard dose of *Feelenhance,* he's been doing fine?"

"I did not know that."

"How do you feel, hearing it now?"

"For how long has he been 'doing fine'?"

"What's that?"

"How long has he been fine?"

"We received the report from the Belair two weeks ago."

"Isn't that rather quick, in view of the problems he has, a bit too soon to say he's doing well?"

Timothy White tapped Avalon's shoe with his own to warn him to stop.

"Of course I'm glad to hear that anyone is doing well, including Dr. Prendergast," Avalon added. "It will be better for him and better for me."

"I gather you once said to him, 'take your meds'."

"Is it wrong to say that?"

"He had gone to you for psychotherapy."

"You were just saying that doing psychotherapy with people who carry this diagnosis was a problem. I made that remark about his taking his meds before he came to me for psychotherapy."

"Why did you tell him to take his meds?"

"Because of the way he behaved. I suppose there's no reason why you should know this: Over the last year he has deliberately woken my wife and me up hundreds of nights by blowing his car horn under our window and making other noises, damaged and defaced our fences, yelled obscenities at us on the street, gouged and disfigured our garden bench, scratched the car and punctured its tires . . . ."

"That's hard to believe."

"I know that. But if he has done it, and if he knows what he's doing . . ."

"Those allegations are irrelevant here."

"Except that my being here is one more thing he's done. But what he's done is irrelevant, and his character is irrelevant, not to mention any diagnosis that I think appropriate. Can't you hear that I'm put in an impossible position, and that he's a dangerous man?"

"That sounds paranoid."

"It's easy for you to dismiss what he does. I wish I could. Why did you ask what I felt on learning that he's better? Did you assume that it would bother me, that I'm so arrogant I'm motivated by vanity more than by a concern that someone should be treated fairly, that I would be unhappy to hear about his improvement at the hands of someone else?"

"I don't think," Dr. Lee said to Timothy White, who under the table was stepping hard on Avalon's shoe, "this is a case where we would take away his license."

On receiving a telephone page, Lee absented himself from the room.

"Don't argue with him," White muttered.

"My lawyer's telling me to keep my mouth shut, and not saying much himself," Avalon muttered back, though Lee had not yet returned. "It's not real."

"They don't have much on you except the diagnosis, and they're not supposed to take action on diagnoses alone, as reasonable colleagues can disagree about them. If he gets angry enough, he'll find something else that could be serious."

Lee returned, his face more expressionless than before.

"I doubt," he said to White, talking about Avalon as if he weren't there, "that Dr. Prendergast wants to sue him."

"How would you know that?" said Avalon. "You've made a deal!"

Lee gathered his papers into a brief case.

"Has the Board made a deal with Prendergast?" Avalon persisted. "Did you promise him some sort of action against me in exchange for an assurance that he wouldn't sue, because it wouldn't be a sound case if he tried?"

Speaking again only to White, Lee said, "We'll

render our decision in due course." He liked the word 'render'; he had used it several times.

"We would like to meet with the Board again," said White.

"Why is that, counselor?"

"You say this is principally about Affect Deficiency Syndrome. We didn't know that and would like time to prepare a response to it."

"But you have responded today."

"My client has informed me that there is at least one other psychiatrist who knows Dr. Prendergast who might be in a position to attest that he does not have Affect Deficiency Syndrome, a psychiatrist who also knows the people at the Belair Hospital who have seen Dr. Prendergast and to whom the group at the Belair often refers patients with that diagnosis."

"I'll have to consult with our legal."

"Your legal?" said Avalon, not comprehending.

"Our legal department."

There was no half smile or handshake at Avalon's and White's departure. A show of fake civility was too much at this point even for Lee.

*

The sunlight outside, as bright as an interrogator's lamp, blinded their eyes.

"He was so angry and righteous," said Avalon. "He reminded me of Mao's Red Guards – I saw a program about them on television last night – even the way he shifted from one foot to the other as he 'struggled' with me. I couldn't get anywhere with him."

"He slapped down everything you said. I'm glad

you didn't say more. You'll want to be careful with anything you say."

"Wouldn't you speak up to defend yourself?"

"Depends on whom I'm talking to. In these situations I wouldn't say anything, even to my wife, that I wouldn't be prepared to see the next day in the *Boston Globe*. You're dealing with colleagues and competitors eager to show how virtuous they are at your expense, and who will never admit that has anything to do with it."

"Is it this bad among lawyers?"

"A lawyer's work may not always be fun, but we don't have to be nice or pretend to like one another when we don't."

"What do you think The Board is going to do with this sinner?"

"As I said, they don't have much except the matter of the diagnosis, and they're not supposed to take any action on the basis of a diagnosis when there are legitimate reasons for a difference of opinion; something to that effect's in the state regulations that govern their hearings."

". . . the regulations!"

"I thought I said something to you about it during the hearing."

"Not that, exactly, only that they oughtn't to make the diagnosis the issue, not that they weren't allowed to. Why didn't you say something about it then, to him?"

White didn't answer.

"Can I sue the Board if they do something inconsistent with the regulations?"

"You'd have to sue the Commonwealth of Massachusetts. You wouldn't stand a chance. Meanwhile, the Board isn't actually a court. With all these professional disciplinary authorities, once you're drawn into its territory, there aren't many checks on its power. I'll try to secure another meeting with them to present the additional evidence we told them about; if that doesn't work, Helen Keller could see the writing on the wall."

"'If that doesn't work . . . .'" Avalon had not yet fully grasped the point. "They can't refuse to grant another hearing, can they?"

"They can do all sorts of things they couldn't do in court."

"You say 'They'. Lee was the only one there. Should others have been there too?"

"As I say, they can do pretty much what they like. Perhaps one of them will relent and think twice about what they're doing."

"That's the last thing I want to rely on. People generally don't forgive those they've treated badly. Think of the consequences if they did: they would have to feel bad about themselves. If they don't continue the hearing, and if they go ahead on the basis of what appears to be their thinking now, it will be an injustice."

"That's mere reality. I deal with laws and regulations."

*

It was hard for Avalon to return to the reality he knew. The atmosphere of the hearing, clung to him like an acid fog and remained an irritant.

True horror stories, he thought, take place without moonlight and creaking doors, even under fluorescent light.

When he was home again, Avalon telephoned Mendelson.

"Something's come up; I'm hoping that you can help."

"Of course, Henry . . . Glad to oblige."

Of the two great engines of human motivation – the pursuit of what is inherently gratifying as in love-making or a good dinner, and the regulation of self-esteem – Mendelson, while not above enjoying the former, was driven principally by the latter. It was flattering to be asked for help.

"I can't tell you how good it is to hear that."

"Sounds serious."

"Possibly."

Avalon brought Mendelson up to date.

"What can I do?" asked Mendelson. It was not as gratifying to provide help as it was to be asked for it. The tone of Mendelson's voice gave Avalon the first indication of disappointment.

"You've written about ADS."

"From what you say, your patient doesn't sound like someone with ADS."

"Precisely! I agree. It would be a great help if you would say that. Will you help me out?"

"Help you out? How do you mean?"

"Have a look at the case, and if you think it's not a case of ADS, say something to that effect."

"About the judgment of another psychiatrist . . . to be an expert witness . . . I don't know. I suppose you could send me the information and I'll have a look at it. But it's not the sort of thing I do."

"Thank you, thanks a great deal."

It was several days later, after a number of

unreturned calls, when Avalon reached Mendelson again.

"I don't do forensic psychiatry," said Mendelson, "and I haven't been an expert witness before. I've always regarded it as a way of compensating for not having enough work." It was not only the content of what Mendelson said that was rapidly eroding what remained of Avalon's fragile hope, but the measured tones with which he more typically talked to a patient or a junior trainee.

"Does that mean you don't want to help?"

"It's not that I don't want to . . ."

"You thought he probably wasn't someone with ADS."

For all the care with which typically he added clause upon clause, Mendelson could be sudden and abrupt, particularly when to engage any further posed a threat to his superior position.

"He could be."

"Could be? I don't understand. The last time we spoke you said he didn't have ADS. Why do you think now that he might be?"

"It is admittedly hard to pin down precisely; it's an uncertain area. Something new takes a while to map out."

"I'm not questioning that."

"There is a principle involved, for me, at least."

"What a man will and won't do in the name of principle, as long as he doesn't have to get off his high horse," Avalon thought. He said, "What principle is that?"

"I have believed for some time that our profession ought to stay out of court," said Mendelson. "We train to be helpful to our patients. A court is a choreographed fight. People don't go to court to be helpful to one another."

"Of course; but I need help now, and it isn't a court."

"I doubt that I would do any good."

"You might if you would say that Prendergast doesn't necessarily have Gefühlsarmut Syndrome. The diagnosis appears to be largely a matter of opinion anyway."

"If he's as bad as you say, you don't need a diagnosis. The denizens of the dark are more interesting and more realistic than any nomen-clature we try to attach to them. You could talk about him in plain language: he's cruel and sadistic."

"Others have already set the stage – and the language."

"I'm sorry, Henry . . . Did you hear that Dr. Koestler's dog has died?"

When Avalon failed to reply, Mendelson said, "You have no reaction?"

"I'm overjoyed."

"Don't you have any sentiments?"

*

"That's not the kind of sympathetic remark you're known for with your patients," said Helena when Henry told her what had transpired in his talk with Mendelson.

"No one of true sentiment could have said anything else."

*

"Who was that, dear?" asked Mrs. Mendelson when her husband got off the phone.

"Avalon."

"I overheard just a moment of it; why weren't you more friendly with him?"

"He doesn't have a very prominent position, Andrea; it looks as though he never will."

"I was asking why you weren't more friendly."

"I thought I told you. The cost of friendship would have been to become involved in a problem of his."

When a talk that Mendelson was supposed to give was cancelled because of bad weather, he found himself with time on his hands, and a worm of regret gnawing at his memory of his telephone conversation with Avalon. Avalon was falling out of favor. One colleague had wondered if he had come unhinged. There would be no ill consequence, and no disgrace, if he offered Avalon no help. On the other hand, Avalon probably didn't deserve the fix he was in. He wrote a letter on stationery bearing his letterhead:

In spite of the benefits of a new diagnosis like the Gefühlsarmut, or Affect Deficiency Syndrome, which offers new understanding and points to clinical interventions, a diagnosis, with the crisp, concise picture it affords, is not always adequate to account for complex clinical presentations. When such conditions exist, diagnoses are best used with caution, leaving room for the clinician to proceed on the basis of his experience and clinical judgment whether or not these are entirely consistent with a particular diagnosis.

Mendelson knew that what he had written was a truism, a platitude, but thought it was the best he could do in the circumstances, enough so that he would not have to feel bad for doing nothing. Still, unable able to leave it at that, he posted a note to Avalon by e-mail: "sent the board a note. Keep in mind: paranoids need their paranoia – if Prendergast is in fact paranoid. Let's hope it's something less ominous."

"He may be manic and eccentric, but not nasty like Pendergast," said Henry, showing Helena the letter.

"It is a gesture; it may even help."

When Lee received Mendelson's letter, he read it and filed it.

"Mendelson is always willing to be helpful." Favorable thoughts about Mendelson came spontaneously. He was mindful of Mendelson's professional and academic prominence, and was by nature inclined to respect someone so well established. "If he knew the details of the case, I have no doubt he'd understand why we have to act."

*

That night Dr. Prendergast, flushed with an exhilaration no drug could have provided, gouged the Avalons' garden bench several times, cut the trunk of a sapling dogwood that Helena had recently planted, dragged an ice pick the length of the right side of their car, and left some feces on the steps to Avalon's office. The progress of events was under control and bringing him closer to his goal.

SHRUNK

26

The day brought no relief for Helena. Her mother had lost her way when going to the train station and stopped a pair of policemen to ask directions.

Unsure of her English and tongue-tied, she asked them in Italian: "Dove la stazione?"

When they stared at her blankly, she tried again in French: "Où est la gare?"

After "Wo ist der Bahnhof?" fetched no reply, she walked off in frustration and got lost.

"Maybe we should teach more foreign languages in our schools," said one officer to the other.

"I don't see why; it didn't do her any good."

After a call from her mother asking for directions, Helena left work to find her and drive her to the Institute for Contemporary Art. When she arrived home, Helena phoned Dr. Boseman, a psychiatrist she had seen in the past, to schedule an appointment.

"Will you come with me to Dr. Boseman?" she asked Henry when she returned home.

Henry was sitting in the living room trying to warm himself with a glass of sherry. He shrugged and agreed to go. Helena assumed that Dr. Boseman would take her side if they met with him together, reinforcing the strength of her arguments. Henry hoped that Dr.

Boseman's office would provide a neutral venue for the kind of discussion that eluded them at home, and help Helena to understand his reluctance to sell the house and move.

*

Boseman's office was in the basement of his home, like an underground cave or the lair of a seer in a folk tale – a genre where the outcomes, Henry recalled, were often unhappy. The impression was supported by Boseman's withdrawn position on a chair in the shadows of a corner mumbling an old pipe.

"You'll have a hard time, won't you," said Boseman as soon as Henry sat down, "when she graduates and is in a position to be more independent?"

Taken aback by the critical nature of the question, after a few moments Henry managed to reply, "Why should that be? I've supported her independence more than her mother, her father, or her former lover ever did. I encouraged her to go ahead with the program she's in and paid her tuition . . . Why do you assume that I would have a hard time with her independence? Are you her white knight?" He didn't say, "Has your judgment been seduced by Helena's good looks?"

Dr. Boseman did not argue; he became thoughtful, the fruit of which was a not very helpful question he asked later in the hour: "Is love possible in these circumstances?" A therapist's neutrality can be a matter of affect, voice, and perspective, as well as the content of what he says; Henry feared that Boseman's questions, not to mention remarks he might have made in conversations with Helena before now, had already done damage that would be hard to reverse.

Helena was of two minds about Henry's exchange with Boseman. While it unhorsed her therapeutic knight, and reminded her of what Henry had done for her, which made her uncomfortable, she admired Henry for standing up for himself. Without the exchange in Boseman's office, the dialogue they had afterwards might never have taken place.

"Shall we try a weekend together?"

"That's a wonderful idea."

"On the Vineyard?"

"Yes."

"It will be off season; it'll have an atmosphere all its own."

"It will."

"Lord knows we need it."

"And deserve it."

"To judge by what's been happening recently, I'm not sure any longer that anyone deserves anything. It's not the way things work."

*

The ferry making its way through the mist, the hidden shore that reluctantly emerged from it, the lonely charm of the island villages out of season, worked their spell on them on their arrival. They stayed in a bed-and-breakfast, an old wooden house with a wrap-around porch, made comfortable inside by the fire in the parlor, upholstered and wooden furniture and an assortment of magazines that looked old even when they weren't. The room smelled of bread and muffins that had been baked for afternoon tea. Freddie was with them and it was all very comforting. The bed-and-breakfast was such a charming facsimile of a home, they felt all the more keenly that they were no longer comfortable in their own house.

They walked along the beach, at this time of year empty of tourists, a few yards from where the sea disappeared in the mist. It recalled for them the quiet pleasures of simply being together which, since they had moved into their house, had too often eluded them.

They tried. They enjoyed the wind in their hair, and the warmth of the inn after dinner when they sat in comfortable old chairs before the hypnotic flickering of the fire. They were more aware of such things than they were of their feelings for one another; they did not want to be aware of feelings that had to do with recent events that had been so disheartening. They had come to the island to leave them behind if they could.

The empty conversation with the hostess was comfortable in the same way as the furniture.

"You're from Boston?"

"Cambridge."

"Of course, you told me. Is it nice to get away?"

"Very."

"I imagine it's quieter down here."

"We're glad it is."

Passionate and unpleasant feelings can intensify when a person goes to bed, when distractions are put aside with the books and glasses that are left on the bedside table, and one feels vulnerable. Then unresolved anxieties come out from wherever they've been tucked away to keep one awake, or startle one out of a sound sleep in the middle of the night. There was nothing for Henry and Helena on the island now but the two of them and the space between them, a situation that can be the goal of love or its tomb. An unstable mix of hope and despair forced Helena to break the silence:

"I wish we weren't mired in this, that you had managed to keep us clear of it. I can't help blaming you for it sometimes, though I try not to and I don't really think it's your fault."

She involuntarily shrank from Henry when he put his arm round her. She hadn't anticipated that she would do this. Having done it, she regarded her reaction, because her body had spoken involuntarily, as equivalent to the voice of God. Henceforth she would not let herself deviate from the course her body and her feelings dictated. Neither love nor reason was as clear or as imperative in its authority over her as her own physical reaction that arose spontaneously in her body and was now the mysterious source of her feelings. Its clarity, however temporary, was the only the relief she could find.

She said none of this; yet Henry understood it implicitly and completely, an understanding that expressed itself in the helplessness that suddenly overwhelmed him, the darkness that permeated his thoughts and his perspective on the future. There was nothing more for them to enjoy on the Vineyard. Its charm, which in the past he had enjoyed regardless of the weather, like so much else of late, had become irrelevant.

27

In Cambridge Avalon was under siege. Fully aware now of the threat posed by the Board, he thought of his case all the time, of what he might do to influence it in a favorable direction. He kept a small notebook with him at all times so as not to forget any idea that might be useful in presenting his argument to the Board. Not since the end of a failed relationship some years ago, when he held onto every thought and phrase that might have proved useful in preventing its demise, had he maintained such a relentless focus on a problem. At dinner he would leave the table abruptly in order to scribble down a thought before it was lost, and was too distracted to notice the effect of his behavior on Helena.

Articles he had been writing for professional journals languished. On his desk and on the shelves in his office, piles of paper grew with different versions of the statement he was preparing for his second meeting with The Board. They filled his briefcase, surrounded his computer, and spread as far as the bedside table. Weekend evenings when he and Helena might have gone to a restaurant or the cinema he now spent at his desk in an endless effort to make his argument more convincing, clinging to the hope that The Board would grant a second hearing and there prove sufficiently fair and willing to listen to make his efforts worthwhile. Convinced that Timothy White had been correct, but ineffectual, he determined to take charge of his case himself.

He cleaned his statement to The Board of anything suggesting that he was quarreling with them or that might be interpreted as disrespectful of their authority. In his first experience with The Board he had noticed Lee's impatience; they were unlikely to appreciate a long appeal. Nevertheless, the need to explain himself grew ever more compelling and caused his appeal to grow longer as it got better. The Board's previous refusal to understand motivated him to try all the harder and made it impossible to make his argument lean and short, the sort of thing they might read and think about. His argument grew more impressive, or would be with those willing to be impressed, and all the while it took more out of him.

*

Timothy White succeeded in contacting Dr. Braun, a psychiatrist who was willing to testify that he had some acquaintance with Dr. Prendergast and that while he had never seen Dr. Prendergast as his patient, he had doubts that the diagnosis of Gefühlsarmut Syndrome, or Affect Deficiency Syndrome applied to him. With so little else available, Avalon pinned his hopes on Dr. Braun's support. He knew the people at the Belair who had diagnosed Prendergast; over the last year or so they had referred several patients with ADS to Dr. Braun for treatment. His opinion could not be so easily dismissed.

"Well, that's something," said Helena. "It's one

thing to bully a lone practitioner, quite another to take on two of you."

"I've staked my hopes on that too. But they were so unwilling to listen before."

"You say 'they'; only one of them was there. Perhaps the others will be more reasonable."

"Their not being there may only mean they can't be bothered to listen either, perhaps more so than the one who was there."

"Isn't it the essence of your profession that one listens?"

"We often give our best to our patients, not our colleagues."

"They must assume that what they do to their colleagues doesn't matter very much."

"Either that, or they just can't help it."

*

"Jennifer, you haven't told your husband yet, have you?"

"No."

"Why not?" Prendergast leaned back in the large armchair in his living room and glared at Mrs. Marston as he interrogated her. He believed it was a friendly gesture on his part to see his patients in his living room, but the room was of no help to himself in regulating his own feelings. Her failure to comply with his recommendation, her defiance, as he saw it, made him far angrier than she knew or could imagine. She feared he might be angry with her, but could detect no sign of anger or any other emotion behind the beard. His gaze was intense, but then it always had been.

"It won't be easy."

"You ought to tell him what you've got to tell him. Nine years of not telling him hasn't done you any good."

"We've been married fifteen and a half years; we've been separated for only nine."

"*Only* nine years. All the while living under the same roof. How much longer are you going to linger?"

"I haven't thought of it as lingering."

"I have some doubts about your thought processes. You don't seem to be planning on leaving him. In fact you have no plan at all, although for nine years you've teetered on the brink. You have trouble making decisions, Jennifer, but that's the only way you'll be able to take appropriate action."

"My previous therapist would refuse to tell me what to do when I asked him. He said that I was the one who would have to live with the consequences."

"Perhaps he was a psychoanalyst; they go on as if time didn't matter."

"Is it always better to be quick?"

"It's more effective. When you first came to me you said that you appreciated my forcefulness. It was a relief after the indecisiveness, the unwilling-ness of previous therapists to be down-to-earth and practical and tell you what to do."

"I know, but when I think of what could happen . . ." she said, wringing her hands again.

"Of course there may be consequences. That's what you want."

"I do? I mean, do I have to?"

"Why did you come to me?"

"All those years together. And then there's Johnny."

"Would you stay married just because of your son?"

"He was only recently discharged from the hospital. It's been so hard for him. What if Edward and I part and Johnny can't handle it?"

"It could be useful to him to see that his parents don't helplessly stay locked forever in a hopeless situation, that they're finally able to act."

"I don't know . . ."

"You're resisting. Good-bye."

"You usually mention our next appointment at the end, and you haven't today. Are we meeting again next week at the same time?"

"Let's meet again when you have something to tell me."

"It's not only me, it's Johnny." Mrs. Marston was crying now. "I don't know how he'll take it. Perhaps we should explore it with him."

When Dr. Prendergast refused to reply, she left.

28

The delivery of every letter, regardless of its contents, was for Prendergast akin to the arrival of a visitor interrupting the tedium of his life alone. When he received a letter from the State Licensing Board for Mental Health Professionals, as Dr. Avalon had done, he did not experience the same mixture of curiosity and dread that Avalon felt the day he held a similar envelope in his hands. It was with a feeling of excitement that Prendergast opened his, which was too thick to hold only a letter, a sign that he had been successful in his next objective. The letter informed him that he had been appointed to the Board and asked if he could step in early to replace a physician who, for family reasons, wished to absent herself for the remainder of her term. A calendar of meetings for the rest of the year was enclosed.

Prendergast spent the rest of the day drafting his reply:

> . . . deeply appreciate the honor . . . look forward to working with colleagues for whom I have considerable respect . . . the Board's high purpose . . . to serve the public interest . . . its unique power, unencumbered by the legalistic

procedures which inevitably hamper the work of the courts . . . the virtue of its concerns and its difficult but public-minded work . . . . Unfortunately, I shall have to delay taking up my duties on The Board until one particular case currently before it is resolved. No doubt you know which case it is and understand that, as the complainant, I must recuse myself from The Board's considerations in the matter, despite its importance to me and my strong feelings about it ever since certain competent colleagues came up with my correct diagnosis and pointed the way to my subsequent improvement.

I hope that this delay, necessitated by the ethics we are dedicated to uphold, will not be a serious inconvenience. No doubt you have anticipated it.

Very sincerely yours,
Albert Prendergast MD

"We assumed he understood that we did not expect him to serve before the case was decided," said Cutter, a member of the Board who had not attended Avalon's hearing. "If we needed any evidence that, despite his having been in treatment, he deserves the honor of serving on The Board, he provides it with this demonstration of his scruples,"

"A good man," said Lee. "I thought he would be; it's why I supported his candidacy. He appreciates the importance of the discovery of Affect Deficiency Syndrome and the need to insure that people benefit from it. And he acknowledges his own affliction; there's nothing like that in what Avalon presented."

"I called Mendelson," said Dr. Wolpert. "He also sees no reason for prohibiting Dr. Prendergast from assuming his position on the Board because of his ADS, and hopes that such an important position's being held by someone carrying the diagnosis will in the long run serve the public good and help to eliminate the stigma that may attach to it."

Drs. Wolpert, Lee and Cutter looked at each other with feelings of satisfaction while they reflected on their civic-mindedness and their devotion to a cause.

"Meanwhile, as for Avalon . . ."

". . . that a colleague should be the victim of his incompetence."

"He needs to be taught a lesson, for his sake and for the public good."

"Shall we . . . we can't take away his license."

"In fact, I doubt the diagnosis can be the basis for any action we take."

"He's unlikely to know that."

"It's a diagnosis that's still being developed; it's not yet in the diagnostic manual. In that sense, he's right: it's not unquestionably established that it exists.

"It's only a matter of time. The manual isn't changed every year. It's bound to fall behind."

"Almost no one reads the state regulations governing the Board. If we impose a mild punish-ment, he'll probably accept it. The alternative would be for him to appeal our decision, which would mean appealing it to us, or to sue, and his lawyer's smart enough not to bother with either of those options."

"A reprimand?"

"If we play it safe, just a cautionary letter. I don't see how they would dare object to that. We can include some disciplinary measure – that he has to submit to a year of supervision, or take a course – something of that sort. It'll cost him some money – like a fine."

"His lawyer asked for a second meeting. He says there's another psychiatrist who's seen Dr. Prendergast, well known to and respected by the group at the Belair, who would testify that Prendergast doesn't have ADS."

"I shouldn't bother; we don't know who this new man is; if it's someone chosen by Avalon he may not really believe in the diagnosis."

"The fact remains that Avalon failed to diagnose ADS in his patient."

"That's what's unforgivable."

"And dangerous."

"What you've suggested is about as kind as we can be to him."

"It is kind, though I doubt he'll appreciate it."

"In any case, I don't see why we should go out of our way to do him any favors. It wouldn't serve the public interest."

29

"You moved out!" echoed Prendergast when Mrs. Marston told him what she had done. "You and your husband are separated. Congratulations! You were finally able to rise to the level of action. From the look of you, you don't yet seem to fully appreciate what you've accomplished."

"Johnny is taking it hard, Dr. Prendergast."

"You've got to expect some sort of reaction."

"At first he was angry all the time, walking about the house banging things and slamming doors, looking sullen and not responding when I tried to speak to him. When he did talk, he was sarcastic and quick with me."

"Unpleasant, but not serious."

"He broke a few things. Then he ran away. I haven't seen him for several days; he hasn't seen his father either."

"He'll be back."

"I'm glad to hear that. It's a help to someone as uncertain as I am. In the past when he ran away he got into bad company and took drugs."

"He'll be back. Where else does he have to go?"

"I'm afraid, Dr. Prendergast."

"Fear is the wrong emotion at this juncture."

"I can't help feeling it."

"The situation needed a breakthrough."

"I hope you're right," Mrs. Marston wrung her hands. "I so hope you're right."

"Would you want to go back to things the way they were?"

"I don't know; maybe. If . . ."

"We have to stop now."

30

Avalon received notification that a second meeting with The Board requested by Timothy White had been denied.

"It's the curse of the profession: facile, contemptuous, dismissive judgment. Not just this in this situation; it happens too often in conversations among colleagues, in their attitudes towards one another."

"The worst of it is they've convinced themselves they're doing good by it, " said Helena.

"Virtue is a good platform for aggression. All those combustible heretics over the centuries went up in flames for what they believed were good causes."

"If we aren't going to burn, one way or another, we had better move away from here."

"I still don't like the idea of running away just because the creep next door is being difficult."

Helena now had doubts about Henry. She thought it unkind to say anything about them, but this time, after Henry had again brushed aside her pleas that they should move away together, kindness did not extend to inhibiting herself in acting on her doubts. She left a note behind.

"Henry, this isn't easy – I'm moving out with Freddie whether you are or not. Let me know if you change your mind."

To Prendergast's profound gratification, Helena moved out of the Adams Street house and taking Freddie with her. She went to stay with her mother.

Henry's refusal to move in the face of Prendergast's relentless harassment had first frustrated and then alarmed her, and generated thoughts that she was unable to suppress. She harbored new suspicions that Henry's early success had been the unearned benefit of easy times rather than the hard-won fruit of the years he had worked to acquire what they had, and even if he had earned his success, he might yet turn out to be one of those men destined to have bad luck. She wasn't sure that she ought to stick around to find out, or wait for the last chapter of an increasingly unpleasant story whose outcome she could influence only if she were prudent enough to act before it was too late. As Dr. Boseman might have said, it was a matter of taking care of herself.

She had never quite forgot the advice, offered by her mother in her relentlessly cheerful, sing-song voice, that it was as easy to find a rich man as an unlucky one. Helena was surprised, on arriving at her mother's, to find that her reaction was not altogether sympathetic. Her mother's was evidently anxious at the prospect of Helena's having no man at all, although, in view of Henry's recent difficulties, she shared her doubts about Henry.

"At least it hasn't been boring," said Helena, appealing to what had often seemed her mother's chief interest when it came to other women's men. She had

171

made sure that her own lock-jawed husband had been cautious, dull and safe. Of Helena's men, her favorite had always been, and still was, William Bassett, whose womanizing and risk taking, not to mention the hint of barely controlled aggression whenever he stood with his large frame constrained in the enclosed space of a room. He had represented the kind of excitement that she herself had been careful not to marry. Years after Helena had ceased to have anything to do with him, he still would still drop by her mother's for small loans and be given odds and ends of furniture that Helena's mother no longer needed and readily gave to him.

When Helena was little, her mother, unable to bear what she felt at the sight of tears on Helena's face, laughed when her daughter cried. Helena had grown up preferring not to make her fear and sadness known to others, better still, not to be aware of them herself. The difficulty of living by that principle had made her increasingly uneasy in the presence of Henry's distress. Her mother's cheerful voice was familiar if not quite comforting.

*

Alone now, Avalon left a message with Waring suggesting another lunch, despite the tension between them in their last meeting,.

Mendelson had just stopped by at Waring's office, where they heard Avalon's message as it played on the answering machine. In the past Waring had received several referrals from Avalon, sending him few in return. Waring reckoned there were still better sources elsewhere, Mendelson himself, for example, whom he was recently seeing more of, and who was closer to the centers of power at The Belair.

"He's in a spot of trouble," said Mendelson.

"A good man, but a lightweight," said Waring.

Neither Mendelson nor Waring had a clear idea of precisely what that meant, but they let it stand as definitive, a judgment that would enable them to ignore Avalon and make light of him without any twinges of **either** guilt or doubt. Avalon's message went unanswered.

*

Posters for by-elections to the City Council to fill places that had been unexpectedly vacated appeared that week on fences and lawns in the neighborhood of Adams Street. Among the usual names of Griswold, Kerrigan, and Chaney, who had figured in local politics for years, there now appeared posters for Prendergast showing the forced smile with which he had charmed the mediator.

Seeing one of these posters newly planted in front of Prendergast's house, Avalon stopped at a real estate broker's office a block away.

31

Johnny Marston was found wandering the streets disheveled and babbling to himself. When the police officer who stopped him asked who he was and where he was going, Johnny stared straight ahead neither looking at the officer nor away from him, as his face broke into a smile. He mumbled a handful of incomprehensible words, and let out a scream that had no evident meaning or purpose. The styrofoam cup he absent-mindedly crushed in his hand spilled its contents over his clothes. He didn't seem to notice.

"We'll take you to a hospital. There's one nearby."

The policeman took Johnny to the Middlesex County Hospital, the psychiatric hospital not far from where they had found him, where his interaction with the admitting physician at the hospital was not much different from what it had been with the policeman; the contents of a second cup spilled over Johnny and the doctor's desk while Johnny gazed out the window with a fixed smile that, whatever it represented, nevertheless looked genuine.

32

The police brought another youth to The Belair Hospital that day. The oval shape of his closely cropped head gave his face a melancholy nobility that lent credibility to the information he gave to the doctor who admitted him.

He was, he said, from a noble and wealthy family in Eritrea who were proprietors of a large estate in the highlands and a house in Asmara. This information was passed to James Lauder who invariably introduced himself as Chief Resident at the Belair Hospital to new patients, colleagues he spoke with on the phone, and others he met at parties, nearly everyone except the women in the cafeteria who gave him food and drink, to whom he said nothing. Lauder took this information about the newly admitted patient seriously.

"Barlow," he said to his favorite second year resident. "There's a new patient for you."

"I thought I was up next," said Richards, another resident.

Lauder enjoyed a passing reflection on his sensitivity in not telling Richards outright that he preferred not to assign such an important patient to a first year trainee.

"I thought this patient and Barlow would be a good

match," he said, an explanation Richards accepted because he did not understand it and because Lauder, also a trainee but two years ahead of him, seemed, in the hierarchical society of the hospital, a person of august stature.

"He's from Eritrea, but definitely VIP, one of the important families there," Lauder informed Barlow when Richards had left the room. "Go walk him through the process at admitting."

*

"Do you have any insurance?" asked the clerk in the admitting office.

"Insurance?"

"A company that will pay your bills here?"

"No."

"Will your family pay?"

"Yes."

"Are you sure?"

"Don't worry," Lauder murmured to the clerk. "He's from a prominent family in Asmara. They'll pay."

"Welcome to the Belair Hospital," the clerk said, duly impressed.

"It's fortunate you've come here," said Lauder as he and the patient went upstairs to the unit where he would stay during his hospitalization. "This is one of the best hospitals in the area." He meant to differentiate the Belair, a teaching hospital with university affiliation, from state hospitals and small private clinics. The patient kept his appreciation, such as it was, and his confusion to himself; his expression remained unchanged.

"Had you ended up somewhere else, they might not have understood."

The patient looked knowing and distinguished when he nodded. It was easy to believe that he understood.

Barlow, the most junior and therefore most cautious of the staff so far involved with the Eritrean patient, telephoned Mendelson, who held a senior position on the hospital's teaching staff. Barlow feared that if a mistake were made with the Eritrean patient, it would be held against him even if he weren't responsible.

"From one of the most distinguished families in Eritrea?" Mendelson repeated when Barlow reached him. "It's perfectly all right to have admitted him. Now that he's there, he may need special attention. If you're the resident following him, you may want to read up on Eritrea. There could be cultural factors you ought to know about. I'll drop by later and have a look at him." Barlow felt the importance of the case – the most gratifying experience of the week so far – envelop him in a matter that also involved Mendelson and Lauder, placing him among the big boys. It was rare now for Mendelson personally to interview an inpatient, and the first time he had spoken to Barlow directly.

33

"This may be of some concern to us," said Dr. Cutter at a meeting of the state Licensing Board for Mental Health Professionals. "We've received a complaint about someone who will soon be joining us as a member of The Board. I've sent you copies of the material, including Dr. Prendergast's reply.

"The complaint, filed by Mrs. Jennifer Marston, a former patient of his, alleges that Dr. Prendergast would not listen to her, forced his opinions on her while ignoring and dismissing what she said, and pressed her to leave her husband, which in turn precipitated a relapse in her son's condition."

"Her son was ill before," said Dr. Lee, "with prior hospitalizations."

Cutter read from the complaint: "'Since I have been seeing Dr. Prendergast and following his advice, my son's condition has deteriorated . . .' I would think that her son's case, as you say, is a pre-existing condition. And it's irrelevant – her son wasn't Dr. Prendergast's patient, she was." Cutter resumed his reading of the complaint. "'. . . as well as my marriage.' Also irrelevant."

"She didn't go to him for marriage counseling."

"The diagnosis appears to be correct."

"It isn't questioned."

"As for the treatment. . . . '10 mg Fluoxetine BID, intermittent psychotherapy as needed once every few weeks . . . talked about her marriage . . . .' She writes: 'the medication he prescribed was the one thing that was helpful to me while it lasted.' I don't see anything that's out of order. And her marriage did get his attention. Nothing sounds inappropriate."

"He might have used more of a cognitive and behavioral approach."

"For all we know he did; I believe that's Dr. Prendergast's preferred approach. He doesn't like to waste time analyzing ephemeral mental activity. In any case, I don't see that anything is sufficiently amiss for us to take action."

"In all conscience I don't see how we could."

"Dr. Prendergast's conclusion, that the patient failed to respond to treatment, seems correct."

"It does happen, unfortunately."

"There is nothing incorrect in the diagnosis or treatment, and the patient failed to respond . . . we're all agreed?"

He dictated into a machine, emphasizing the consonants for the typist's benefit: "Complaint dismissed."

*

"We've been unsuccessful in reaching your family," said the secretary from The Belair's billing office. She had come up to the Eritrean patient's unit to ask him some questions. Tom O'Handlin, her boss in the billing office, was concerned about the accumulating balance.

179

"Can you arrange for them to make some payment?"

The patient nodded his noble head.

"Will you be contacting your family in Eritrea?"

The Eritrean patient nodded again. In his mind he saw a blinding white and gold light spread to where it suffused the entire world, as he had seen the sun fill the wide horizon at home, only this was more brilliant and inspiring. It was easier than ever agree to what the secretary said when he was in this frame of mind; there were no limits to what was possible.

The secretary and O'Handlin dared not disbelieve him and were reassured, until later that afternoon when anxiety finally got the best of O'Handlin. He made a series of phone calls to Asmara. By the fourth call he was shouting the patient's name into the telephone.

"I thought you would be the family. If you're not his family, I assume you've heard of them; they're one of the more prominent families in Asmara."

"Wait please."

O'Handlin waited. There was no way to know what was happening on the other end, but having found someone who didn't hang up on him, he reckoned it was more prudent to wait a few minutes than to hang up in frustration and have to try again.

He had reached a telephone in a café lucky enough to have a phone connection on an unpaved, unnamed street in a nondescript quarter of quarter of Asmara. The man who had answered the phone dutifully asked the men in the café if they recognized the name O'Handlin had given him, and returned to the phone.

"Sorry," he said to O'Handlin. "No one knows them."

"Are they out? Do you know when they'll be back or how I can get in touch with them?"

"They're not here."

"Are you in their house now?"

"No."

A new customer came into the café and café's owner hung up.

34

Angelo had a keen sense of who might be useful to him, a potential he attributed more readily to a successful man. Prendergast was the most successful and respected man he had so far met in his short life, a consideration that overrode any inclination there might have been to punish Prendergast for having failed to keep him out of jail. Prendergast had remained the largest figure in his thoughts, the human bond that for the time being was the strongest. After his release from jail, Angelo made his way back to Prendergast who, for a while at least, had offered him more than anyone before had done.

Another man might have voiced some surprise when Angelo reappeared in his doorway after what had happened. Prendergast kept such thoughts to himself, reckoning there might come a time when Angelo, who had once been so useful to him, would come in handy again. Meanwhile, it cost little or nothing to accept the honor Angelo bestowed on him with his reappearance, and to take up the mentor's role again.

"I'm not sure what I can do for you at this point. Our former arrangements, some of them at least, should be left in the past."

In spite of what had happened, Angelo did not

believe that the doctor's considerable powers were diminished. That he, Angelo, had gone to jail for doing Prendergast's bidding was less important to him than that Prendergast had not, that he had got away scot free.

"You have influence and you know how to do things. I can learn from you."

"I'd love to do something for you right now if I could," said Prendergast in a voice modulated to soften the blow of Angelo's disappointment. He felt entitled to Angelo's compliment, and appreciated it; the boy knew how to behave.

"Wait here a moment." Prendergast went to another room to make a phone call. He came back feeling as benign as Buddha.

"Go see the head nurse at Middlesex Hospital. They're always looking for some mental health aides."

"It's not something I know much about."

"It's not a position that requires a lot of prior training. They'll teach you on the job. In any case, with the low unemployment now it's hard to find people and they're flexible about requirements. It would be a start. Don't worry, it won't be difficult; and you'll be paid."

35

Jennifer Marston learned by a call from the police that Johnny had been re-admitted to the Middlesex.

"How is he?" she asked, desperate to know.

"I don't know about these things, ma'am".

"Did he try to hurt himself?"

"I don't know."

"Was he on drugs?"

"I don't know that either; he acted strange."

"Strange?"

"I can't tell you any more, lady. I'm not the doctor."

"Thank you for talking with me."

The officer was touched by her thanks. He was used to exchanges in which everyone talked brusquely without any of the polite forms and it took him by surprise. Having begun by wishing he didn't have to call her, he regretted now that he couldn't do more for her.

"Hasn't the hospital called you yet?"

Mrs. Marston called the hospital as soon as the policeman rang off. The woman at the switchboard connected her with the nursing station of the unit where Johnny was being held.

Angelo was collecting bags of medical waste for disposal when the phone rang. No one else was there;

and with the initiative he had shown elsewhere, he picked up the phone.

"Who are you?"

"I'm his mother. Am I speaking to his doctor?"

"No, but I work here, on the unit where he's been admitted."

"Can you tell me how he is?"

"I'm not supposed to tell people things like that on the phone."

"I'm his mother. Please understand . . ."

"I would have to take your word for it; I'm not supposed to do that. It would be better if you came in."

"Can you tell me if he's tried to hurt himself?"

"I'm not supposed to do this."

"I'll come in, of course. Can't you tell me anything?"

"The doctors say he needs to be here."

"What are you going to do with him?"

It was a new experience that someone would turn to him for help, and he liked it. He had overheard one or two things the nurses had said earlier and offered that. "They're going to do some tests, to see what to do next."

"Tests for what?"

"It looks like he's had PCP, a lot of it, and who knows what else. They'll want to know what effect it's had on his ability to function."

"Thank you. I'll come in."

*

The secretary from the Belair Hospital's billing office went up to Eritrean patient's unit, where she showed him the address they had for his family in Asmara and asked him if it was correct.

He lifted his head to look at it, took the secretary's pen to make a change in it, and rested his head against the back of the chair. It was a gray day; he closed his eyes and waited for the brilliant gold and white light to return to fill the world and himself.

"Well done!" said the director of the billing office when the secretary returned. "Now we'll get somewhere."

"It's not much of a change," said the secretary. A few letters had been changed in the way the name of the road was spelled. She experimented with different pronunciations.

"We'll see."

"It doesn't look as if you'd pronounce it differently. Whoever was on the phone had no idea where they were or who they were." Looking at the changed address, she added: "They may not even use our alphabet."

"It's still our best bet."

A new bill was sent to the corrected address.

*

"The insurance picture is still unclear. You'll have to give us $5000 as a deposit," said O'Handlin.

"He's been hospitalized here before," said Mrs. Marston. "The insurance has always paid eventually, and we paid any balance. It's my husband's insurance. It's a good policy."

"He may have used up the allotted time."

"If you look into it I think you'll find that his insurance doesn't work that way."

"We can't contact the insurance company on a Sunday. I'm sorry, but we'll need the deposit up front."

"That's a lot for me."

"I'm sorry. We would do the same with everyone."

Mrs. Marston wrote O'Handlin a check for five thousand dollars. "I won't be able to pay any more."

The check slid silently across the desk into a drawer.

The proportions of the rooms at the Belair Hospital, the contemporary furniture that was not stylish but merely economical, the bare walls and polished linoleum floor of the room that Johnny shared, were in themselves enough to make Mrs. Marston despondent.

Johnny seemed hardly to notice his surroundings. He smiled to his mother with a spontaneous, friendly, warm smile of the sort she hadn't seen in years; a moment later his smile was as purposeless and meaningless as his crushing the styrofoam cup had been when the policeman stopped him on the street. That the meaning of the most basic human signals was impossible to decipher, that for all the expression in Johnny's face she could not connect with him, that he happily soiled himself as he hadn't done since infancy, that she couldn't be sure he recognized her, were altogether more than his mother could bear.

*

She visited Johnny regularly – several times a week – waiting for an improvement that no one had yet detected. He increasingly seemed to recognize her, but she was uncertain if he recognized the mother he had grown up with or the woman who now came to visit him. Attempts to talk with him about people and places from the past were unsuccessful. He would seem to listen, smile to no one in particular, and make unintelligible utterances that left his meaningless smile intact.

"Here, take this, Johnny. You never know when you'll need it."

She put fifty dollars in his pocket, not quite trusting that his grip was firm enough to hold onto the money if she left it in his hand. She hesitated a moment, feeling both kind and guilty, then said "this too" – and gave him another fifty dollars.

Johnny's doctors shared Mrs. Marston's suspicion that his condition might not be improving.

"There are times when I fear there's been no improvement at all."

"We've wondered about that too."

"Could he have been permanently damaged?"

"It's possible, if the overdose was large enough and there was an extended period of abuse. But we can't tell that now. We'll have to wait and see."

"That's easier for you to do than it is for me."

*

In a patient lounge on another floor of The Belair Hospital, the Eritrean patient held in one hand the little Red Book of Mao Tse Tung, and in his other hand his penis, with which he sprayed several square yards of two adjoining walls.

"What are you doing?" shouted the attendant who came across him while this was going on.

"Cleaning the world."

"What would your father say if he saw you doing this?" Feeling helpless in the face of such bizarre behavior, the attendant invoked as his ally the first authority that came to mind.

"Son of a bitch."

"What would your mother say?"

"Son of a bitch."

*

"He comes from a prominent and wealthy family. The unusual behaviors we're witnessing may not be misbehavior. They're very likely nothing more than cultural differences," said Mendelson at a case conference held in the hospital that afternoon to decide the disposition of the case.

While that meeting was under way, the Eritrean patient's sister arrived at the Belair where she told the staff that she had just come from Eritrea, something that had happened ten months before. She wore a fake leather coat with a faux fur collar, polyester stretch pants, and spoke angrily to Barlow. Having caught a glimpse of the situation before coming into the lounge, Chief Resident Lauder decided it was a job appropriate for a first year resident and withdrew.

"You don't take good care of him," the patient's sister shouted at Barlow. "He's worse than he was before. You do him no good.

"What did they do to you?" she said solicitously to her brother in a voice that lost none of its shrillness.

189

"What's your name?" she demanded of Barlow. "We're going to call our lawyer."

Barlow urged her to restrain herself.

"Why should I? It's the way it works in this country."

*

During the night shift Johnny walked with the shuffle of a patient on neuroleptics down the corridor to a small staff room located near the nurses' workstation.

Angelo looked up. "You already want more?" Normally he would have led Johnny to a more discreet location, but the other aide on the shift had gone home sick. They would not be disturbed.

Johnny stood there mute, unable to elaborate. Getting himself to the workstation was as much communication as he could manage.

'You're sure? OK."

Angelo produced a small packet of white powder and poured the contents into a piece of folded paper, a wrapping less likely to arouse suspicion.

"You won't tell anyone? You can't, can you? Good man. That's twenty dollars."

Johnny held out a handful of money, unable to do the calculations for a transaction.

"Hard to count, is it?" said Angelo, taking what Johnny had pulled out of his pocket, about twenty-five dollars. "You need more money."

He thought that Johnny nodded, and that sufficed for a reply. Angelo followed him back to his room where he persuaded Johnny to show where his money was kept, and took what was there.

"You're smart," said Cutter, an attending psychiatrist on the inpatient unit of the Middlesex who had stopped by because a nurse had told him of some records that required his signature. "An aide is at the bottom of the ladder. You ought to see about obtaining some credentials."

"You think so?" said Angelo. He admired Cutter for his position, as well as the restrained intensity and rapid delivery with which he spoke at the same time as he signed a week's entries in the charts, the very picture of a sophisticated power over others. Cutter, for his part, found something to admire in Angelo's calm and innocent face, immune to any disturbance from within.

"There are all sorts of credentials now. See what they're offering. You could get some sort of certificate related to mental health."

Seeing an advertisement for an on-line Yellow Pages on the television while he was on duty that night, Angelo looked there under Schools and copied down the telephone number of the New England College of Continuing Knowledge, which offered a range of correspondence courses.

36

Jennifer Marston held a copy of Johnny's psychological and neuropsychological test reports in her hands. The section under the heading "Clinical Implications" had been carefully crafted to equivocate, but did not seem equivocal at all to her: "It is difficult to say at this juncture whether, or to what extent, the current impairment of functions described above will ameliorate with time, or if it represents lasting damage to the brain and a chronic condition. Re-testing at some future date may help to clarify the answer to this question." The recommendation for future testing failed to reassure; the vagueness of "some future date" seemed to her an implicit admission that not much was known about the prognoses in such cases. The hints about possible improvement seemed to her merely pro forma.

She dropped the report on the table, next to the decision of the Board of Mental Health Professionals rejecting her complaint against Prendergast. The first communication robbed her of hope for Johnny, the second of any expectation of justice.

It was too much bad news; there was nothing on which to hang hopes of any kind. She needed to speak to someone. The idea of calling Dr. Prendergast occurred to her and was quickly dropped. She cringed at the prospect of another dialogue of the sort she would most likely have with him.

Edward, her husband, had agreed to move out when Mrs. Marston, following Dr. Prendergast's advice, had forced things to a head.

"Are you planning to see Johnny?" she asked.

"I have been seeing him."

"Oh, good . . . . Edward . . ."

"Yes?"

"Do you want to move back in? You could stay in the apartment above, or we could share an apartment. Shall we give it another chance?"

"I don't think so."

"No? I see."

In the back of a drawer in a bureau in her bedroom were the accumulated bottles of tablets left over from various prescriptions of the past ten years when doctors had tried her, and Jonathan, on diverse medications. She gathered a lethal quantity of old tri-cyclic antidepressants and swallowed them with the help of an eight-ounce glass of gin, topped off with some water to clean the taste in her mouth.

37

After a cursory look at the books and other materials of the correspondence course Angelo felt overwhelmed, until it occurred to him to place an ad for a tutor with the Quickie Job Agency at a local college that listed odd jobs for their students..

Jim Harbin was a year older than Angelo, but with his long, gangly frame, the forward tilt of his walk and a quizzical expression in his face displaying curiosity and vulnerability, he looked younger than Angelo, whose development appeared to have culminated at an early age. Lacking as yet a perspective on the future, Angelo was prepared to use what he already had rather than undergo the ordeals of further development. Jim Harbin was no match for him when the two met to do business

Angelo copied out the questions from the take-home exam on a note pad and brought them to his tutorials with Harbin. He was pleased with himself for the way he listened, regarding his patience as a sign of manly reserve, while Jim provided him the answers and told him more than he cared to know.

Angelo had a keen eye for others' vulnerability, and Jim Harbin didn't hide his.

It was evident in the earnestness with which he strove

to teach what he knew, in the hesitant embarrassment with which he accepted payment for his time.

"Do you want some?" Angelo asked one night at the end of a tutorial, rolling a small bag of his goods across the table.

"You've got some to spare?"

"I have to ask you to pay for it."

"Yeah, of course." The money Jim Harbin had just received crossed the table again on its way back to Angelo.

After his exams, Angelo's relationship with Jim continued, though with less regularity and minus the instruction. When he obtained his certificate, he was moved to a daytime job with a modest increase in salary.

38

Near the end of his campaign for city council, Prendergast launched an attack against the weakness and ineffectiveness of councilwoman Chaney, who had until then thought of Prendergast as an acquaintance and a fellow liberal. In the election for seats on the city council, Dierdre Chaney was the one he reckoned he could most easily defeat. By the narrowest of margins, Prendergast took her seat on the city council.

Prendergast enjoyed the creaking of his shoes on the old wooden floors of the City Hall when he arrived for his first council meeting. He ran into Jeremy Smith who had chaired the meeting of the Cambridge Zoning Board when the fence between Prendergast's and Avalon's properties was considered.

"Did things work out satisfactorily between you and your neighbor?" Smith asked.

"I never did get the fence I was supposed to."

"You didn't?"

"I had virtually forgotten about it – I don't like nursing grudges – but now that you remind me . . . I don't suppose there's much I can do."

"Nothing that isn't cumbersome. You could go to court of course. Wait, I remember now . . . there was a new fence in the drawings for the addition that he submitted for a variance. In that case, strictly speaking, he would have to have provided that fence, along with anything else that appears in the drawings."

"I'm not so small-minded that I'd remember something like that off-hand without something to remind me. Now that it's come up, however, thanks for the thought."

Prendergast went downstairs to the room in the cellar of the City Hall where the drawings for variances were filed. He asked Vincent Lazarro, Principal Inspector for the Zoning Board, to pull the drawings that had been submitted for the variance the city had granted to Avalon.

"If I remember correctly," Prendergast said, "what he built isn't entirely according to the drawings that were submitted with his application for a variance."

The drawings showed an "Existing Fence" with no indication that it was to be replaced. No room for complaint there. The new fence Avalon had built left him ahead of the game, as far as fences were concerned. But the bushes the architect had drawn near the office door had never been planted, and the brick steps on the drawings had materialized as wooden ones, a decision made at the time because they were a better match for the style of the house.

"He hasn't done what, in these drawings, he promised he would do," said Prendergast, turning the drawings so that Lazarro could more easily see them.

"Did you raise these points at the meeting of the Zoning Board when the variance was granted?"

"No . . ."

"Normally, that would have been the time to raise objections. It's what those meetings are for."

"My first inclination is to trust people. I trusted that my neighbor would do what he indicated in his drawings."

"What do you want us to do now? He couldn't be made to take down the addition over something like this."

"He uses it as an office."

"That's entirely legal."

"If what's constructed conforms to the drawings accepted by the city. In this case it doesn't."

"Very well, we'll communicate with him."

*

After a letter requesting a time, and a telephone call to confirm it, Vincent Lazarro called on Avalon at his house on Adams Street.

"Are you aware that your property, since the addition was constructed, isn't in compliance with the requirements that accompanied the city's granting of the variance?"

"No, I'm not. How is that?"

"The drawings on the basis of which the variance was granted show a brick staircase to the door of the addition and bushes planted as part of the landscaping."

"Wooden stairs are more compatible with the rest of the house, which as you can see is made of wood. As for bushes, I don't remember any talk about that. Architects put them in their drawings to make them look prettier. Anyhow, they wouldn't grow under these trees."

"They may still be a problem. I'm trying to think of what we could say to Dr. Prendergast. He seems determined, and he has the regulations on his side. I'll look into it and let you know."

*

"It's only a couple of bushes which in any case you couldn't see," Lazarro explained to Prendergast, who had returned to his office. "As for the stairs, I imagine it would be hard to see them too from your side of the fence."

"The present situation constitutes an unfulfilled commitment to the city."

Prendergast ignored the evident reluctance with which Lazarro asked: "What do you want us to do, Dr. Prendergast?" As far as he was concerned, Lazarro had no choice but to ask it, not only because he, Prendergast, was a taxpayer; he was now a city councilor as well.

"Isn't it legally proper for you to tell him that because he hasn't fulfilled the specifications filed with the city, he can not practice in the office in his home?"

"I don't know."

"Do you mean to say that the inspector's office, the city itself, is impotent and can't do anything when a citizen fails to live up to legally binding commitments?"

"I'll write a letter."

The next day Avalon received it:

Dr. Avalon:
    It has come to our attention that the bushes and the brick stairs to the entrance of the new addition to your house on Adams Street

indicated in the drawings you provided when applying for a variance, are not part of the final construction. Until this matter is corrected, you cannot practice as a physician in the office you have newly installed in your addition.

Respectfully,
Vincent Lazarro

He did not know if the city had the authority to prohibit Dr. Avalon from practicing in his home office. Home offices were legal in Cambridge, but Lazarro was under pressure. If perchance the letter was not altogether legitimate, he told himself, Dr. Avalon's interest in the matter was great enough that he would do what he had to do to straighten things out; in the long run, no lasting harm would be done. These thoughts very nearly quieted his conscience.

*

"I'm going to ignore it," Avalon said to Helena, whom he had called to talk about the letter from Lazarro. She was still the person he felt closest to, despite their separation.

"Could a bailiff come to the house and insist that you close your office during an appointment with a patient?"

"I doubt they would do that. It would be bad publicity, bad enough so that even the city wouldn't want it. There will probably be further exchanges of letters."

"Not indefinitely. Something else is bound to follow – a fine perhaps."

"There must be a limit to how far they'll go with something like this. If they push hard enough there will have to be a hearing and that could bring unpleasant publicity for everyone. Imagine the headline: *City Closes Doctor's Office Over A Bush*. They probably sent this letter because Prendergast badgered them; I doubt they'll go out of their way to do much more for him."

"Why bother to find out? He's on the City Council now."

"He is?" Prendergast's election to the city council was news to Avalon. Prendergast seemed to possess infinitely larger forces that were campaigning on several fronts, with no less a goal than his unconditional surrender and destruction. "That's not good."

"Aside from that, he's obsessed with you."

"We're supposed to be colleagues," said Avalon, with a small sarcastic laugh – all he could muster.

"You're more successful than he is, and younger. He resents you on both counts. For a while now he's been trying to resemble you. When you cut your beard, he cut his. We got a garden bench, then he got one – of a sort. We had a child, he 'adopted' a 'little brother'. Meanwhile he's doing everything he can to damage and eliminate you. He's trying to replace you. Don't wait for him to do it . . . Oh Henry, we're arguing about this as if we were still together."

"I don't mind that as much as you do."

On the way out the door after the phone call Avalon saw Prendergast's campaign poster, left over from the election, still standing in front of his house. He stopped by at a real estate broker's office a block away.

39

Savoring his recent successes, and the anticipation of Avalon's imminent defeat, Prendergast worked with new-found inspiration and energy on a manuscript he wrote in rough draft in a month and a half: *The Paranoid's Guide to Modern Psychiatry.*

"Are you sure you want that title?" asked his publisher.

His prudent question failed to temper Prendergast's new-found ambition. The same energy that enabled him to work at a fevered pitch made him confident of his choice for the title and about the added dimension to his life that included the roles of author and politician.

"Many people are afraid of the profession," he explained to his publisher, "or inclined to mistrust it. That title that will appeal to them. The market for mistrust is considerable, and untapped. The entire subject needs a bold and systematic reworking of its theory and clinical approach in order to clear out the debris of past mistakes."

His publisher thought the approach sufficiently provocative to enhance sales.

*

"We're setting up a clinic," said Dr. John Kyle, medical director of the Belair Hospital, "so that we can provide a fuller range of treatment for substance abuse. The clinic would be held two days a week, perhaps, with some sort of walk-in on the other days."

"It will need to be staffed," said Mendelson,

"There's this fellow Prendergast at Middlesex County Hospital who could bring a new angle to it."

"What's the new angle?"

"Affect Deficiency Syndrome and substance abuse," said Mendelson, who liked the idea that a diagnosis in which he had specialized would have a clinic devoted to it, but thought it a good idea that he should have some control or influence in the new enterprise.

"He's published one or two papers on the potential for substance abuse among those who carry the diagnosis. He comes with OK references from The Middlesex where he's been a clinic director."

"He may be the only psychiatrist there on the late shift," Mendelson demurred, "supported by a social worker."

"Still, we'll have to give him a similar title."

"Are his papers any good?" asked Mendelson.

"No more than other papers on ADS that link all sorts of things with the same diagnosis. But they do enhance his CV; it's a cut above the CVs of others working with substance abusers."

Mendelson stiffened with concern about how Prendergast might invade his academic niche and impinge on his own position at The Belair.

"It would be good to have more than one person with a special interest in ADS." Kyle, though less well known in other cities than Mendelson, was nevertheless the division chief and spoke with the authority of the one who decided such things.

Picking up Mendelson's concern, he added, "I doubt you'd want to see lots of substance abuse patients."

"No thank you."

"With your new prominence, traveling for speaking engagements, you may not want to overload your schedule with patients."

"Thank you for your understanding." Mendelson's initial anxiety subsided.

"Prendergast could take on a substantial number of patients who carry diagnoses of either substance abuse or ADS. We'll write that into his contract. It should be a good fit."

*

Prendergast's anticipations of his forthcoming publishing accomplishments were followed by day-dreams of academic advancement, television appearances, and greater influence – enhanced by his new position on the City Council – over his environment generally.

When it became clear, after a series of complaints by patients and their families, that Prendergast's relationship with the Middlesex County Hospital had soured to a point where he would be let go before he had quite secured the move to The Belair, none of the standard ways of describing the event – such as being 'laid off' – was acceptable to him. Under threat of legal action the hospital agreed to let him go and to say nothing more in future letters than that his departure was mutually agreed to as part of a necessary restructuring. The arrangement left him with an untarnished record.

Prendergast did not suffer the weakness of not believing in himself. He was reasonably confident that with credentials that were still valid and a willingness to articulate sincerely held ideals and attitudes, he would secure another position. To protect himself against any suspicions that might arise in the future about his departure from the Middlesex Hospital, he lobbied indirectly for a farewell reception in recognition of his years of service to the Middlesex, and his recent contributions in promoting the diagnosis and treatment of Affect Deficiency Syndrome. Cookies and coffee would be served in the hospital's auditorium, after two or three tributes by colleagues and staff and a brief video in remembrance of his time at the Middlesex County Hospital.

*

Henry Avalon had not vanished from his screen – had not even moved to its periphery. From his position on the City Council, Prendergast expected that he could now more effectively see to the enforcement of restrictions prohibiting Avalon's use of his addition as an office. He had been careful not to mention yet the brick pathway that also appeared on the drawings Avalon's architect had originally submitted with the application for a zoning variance. He expected that after a few months of pressure Avalon would replace the existing wooden steps with brick and plant the bushes indicated in the drawings, though any bushes planted there were sure to die under the large trees overhead. When Avalon had done as he would be made to do, Prendergast would then bring up the matter of the hundred-foot-long brick walk, apologizing for having overlooked it before, but insisting once again that the city's zoning regulations had to be respected and complied with. That would involve an additional expense for Avalon of somewhere between five and ten thousand dollars and cause him further delay in resuming his practice in his home office. He would have to rent an office elsewhere – another expense, an appropriate consequence for having failed to put up the right kind of fence.

Now when Prendergast whistled at night and committed other acts of harassment, it was no longer done with the spontaneous hatred and unmeasured venom of before; it was more deeply savored and elaborate, mixed with the exultation of revenge fulfilled.

Prendergast's rise did not go unnoticed in the local press. An article about him appeared in the local Tab, then in the Boston dailies. He was interviewed by an eager young journalist who wrote an admiring article about this local statesman, physician and soon-to-be author. They came with photographers to take pictures of him and his house. On seeing the gaping hole in the fence in front of the house – not the new fence between his property and Avalon's that Avalon had built, but the one that ran along the sidewalk and whose dilapidation had never bothered Prendergast – the disheveled appearance of the yard, and the way evergreen trees and bushes entirely covered the windows on first floor, as they were destined to do on the second, they decided not to bother with photographs of the house.

Avalon put his house up for sale.

40

Unlike the photojournalist, Walter Tremolo had no inhibitions about photographing Prendergast's house. He carried his cameras with him in his peregrinations in and about the city, taking daytime and nocturnal pictures of birds, moths, reflecting puddles and buildings, until he had accumulated a personal library of twenty years' worth of still and video pictures of the life and texture of the city. He still liked to sit on a bench in the park on Adams Street taking pictures of the children and their mothers, and of the park surroundings. Small, surrounded by mature trees and pleasant houses, the park on Adams Street was a favorite location where he would rest during his nocturnal wanderings – the night was tender there – enjoy its peace and quiet when it was empty, and imagine what went on behind the windows of the surrounding homes.

It was in the park one day that Tremolo read in an abandoned newspaper about the recent successes of Dr. Prendergast, whose house had always been a source of frustration on account of the trees that grew so close to it he could barely tell at night if lights were on inside. In the park at night he had lately been hearing the sounds of loud whistling, a car horn, and car doors slamming at unusually late hours, always coming from the vicinity of the same one or two houses. They had made him aware of another creature who, like himself, was often up late and engaged in unusual activities. He might have been inclined to think of Dr. Prendergast as a kindred spirit had Prendergast not spoiled the park's nighttime tranquility.

Avalon's house had also been a focus of his interest. The shades of the windows facing the park were not always drawn and Tremolo had from time to time glimpsed what was going on inside. In his distant, uninvolved way he had come to feel a degree of attachment to the Avalons. Like a naturalist studying the local fauna, he was equally interested in the unpleasant aspects of Prendergast's house and the more pleasant prospect of the Avalons', and he might have remained disinterested had he not overheard some local gossip in the park one afternoon.

"Did you hear about the people in those two houses?" said a woman to her friend. They shared a bench in the park on Adams Street as they watched their children play.

"Are they connected in some way?"

"They're part of the same story, though one of them probably doesn't want to be. Rumor is, the one who lives in the house on the left has been causing trouble for the family that lives in the house on the right."

"How?"

"Making noise, damaging property and puncturing car tires."

"How unpleasant!"

"'Unpleasant?' You talk like the Queen. I wonder what they did to provoke it."

"Why must they have done something to provoke it?"

"Why else would anyone do things like that?"

Tremolo understood now the cause of the sounds he had heard coming from the vicinity of Prendergast's house for the last several months, and understood why a *For Sale* sign had recently been planted in front of Avalon's house. He had seen a shadowy figure moving about, but had no way of knowing at the time what was happening, or that anything was amiss. He might have inadvertently photographed Prendergast in the act of damaging his neighbor's property but until now he would no more have thought of intervening than the producer of a nature film would try to prevent a raptor seizing its prey while he photographed them.

But now the Avalons might move away. Even the most isolated individuals form attachments of the kind that suits them, defend those ties, and find the prospect of losing them disturbing. Should the Avalons move, it would change the environment, the human ecology of his favorite corner of the city. That was a prospect that could motivate Walter Tremolo to do things he wouldn't ordinarily do.

That night in the Adams Street park, with a keener interest and from a closer position than in the past, he photographed and recorded the sounds of Prendergast entering Avalon's driveway where he stopped for a few moments next to their car. The camera followed Prendergast as he returned to his own property, blew his car horn under the Avalons' bedroom, and tossed something over the fence. It caught him again after he went upstairs, leaned out his window and whistled shrilly for half a minute or so.

*

Tremolo went first to the local Tab on the assumption that, having already published an article about Prendergast as an up-and-coming Cambridge politician, they would be interested to know more about him. The man he spoke to in the newsroom put everyone who came to his desk through an initial screening that took account of a person's clothes, style and general appearance.

Walter Tremolo's appearance, with his clothes hanging loosely on his slight frame, and hair that looked as if it had been brushed the day before, caused the man in the newsroom to regard Tremolo as someone insignificant – a man without credentials – to be got rid of quickly.

"Sorry, we don't accept unsolicited pictures."

"They're pictures of someone your paper's already done an article about."

"Unless we were going to do another . . ."

"You might do that if you saw what I have here. They're pictures of Prendergast, the city councilor."

"Oh yes, we did an article on him. Sorry you didn't bring them in earlier."

"These pictures could be the basis for an entirely new story about him."

"Sorry."

*

As Tremolo made his way from the newspaper's offices to the police station, Cambridge looked grayer than usual in the day's dying light. He looked forward to when black night would replace the gray and soften the wintry appearance of the town at dusk on streets that didn't have enough trees.

The officer on duty at the reception desk in the police station made an assessment of Tremolo similar to the newspaperman's. He did not know what to make of the material Tremolo offered to show him. It was different from what he usually dealt with, peculiar, and carried in a paper bag. That and Tremolo's appearance led the officer to disregard him as the male equivalent of a bag lady.

"Are you a private detective," he asked for the sake of thoroughness, dimly aware of the likely answer and the insult implicit in the question.

"No. But this may be a police matter."

"That would normally involve some sort of robbery or violence."

"I'm not sure, but there may be destruction of property, certainly disturbance of the peace."

"There *may* be *some* destruction of property? What kind of disturbance of the peace, where, when?"

"Between two houses . . ."

"Between two houses – what kind of location is that?"

The officer's harsh, contemptuous voice was too much for Tremolo. Defeated in his attempts with the press and the police, he wandered the city until he got to the park on Adams Street at a time when the children and their mothers had already gone home, and high above the park the late afternoon sun gilded the treetops. He swung open the waist-high gate and sat down on an empty bench.

He was the only one there when Parsons left

Avalon's office after an appointment, crossed the street and entered the park. Parsons was in the habit, weather permitting, of spending a few minutes there after his appointments with Avalon.

Had Parsons entered the park first, Tremolo would not have sat near him. Parsons had no such inhibition.

"You've got some pretty fancy gear." Parsons appreciated fine cameras.

"Do you live in that house you came out of?"

"I see a doc there."

"Do you know about cameras?"

"A bit. I'm using them for a project at the college."

"What's the project?"

"I have to find something with local color."

"You haven't found it yet?"

Having been brushed off by the press and the police, Tremolo was more eager than he would typically have been to talk with Parsons.

"I have something that might interest you." He handed Parsons the large manila envelope.

41

It was not uncommon for staff physicians to change jobs in a city that was serviced by more than a dozen hospitals. With his manuscript in press, Prendergast brought more to the table than when he had sought earlier jobs. It seemed only appropriate now that The Belair – a teaching hospital – should be interested in him.

He had secured an interview with Cobb.

"I believe in learning from my patients," said Prendergast.

"What have you learned?"

"There's a humility in realizing that one can learn from one's patients."

"There is, yes. I gather from what you say that you've had occasion to reap the benefits of that."

"I've seen a variety of patients who have had all sorts of experiences and brought in all sorts of information.

"Information?"

"It's given me an appreciation of the variety of problems that people have, as numerous as the ways in which a man can make a living."

"That is an unusual perspective."

"I think I've also learned something about the

nature of authority and how to deal with it. That can be helpful, in therapy as elsewhere."

"That's not talked about enough. We have a group for a few of the hospital's staff members that's just starting up, colleagues who share an interest in what makes for effective leadership. We can always use novel ideas. It's important to keep psychiatry up to date, to make it new."

"I couldn't agree more."

*

Word reached Avalon that Prendergast had obtained a position at The Belair, a teaching hospital with a university affiliation, a more prestigious institution than The Middlesex.

"He must have fooled a lot of people to have had the jobs he's had in the past," Helena said in disbelief, "or he was better once. It's hard to imagine why anyone would hire him now."

"He may be deteriorating without its being obvious. Paranoids can be smart. He wears the right clothes, says more or less the right things when he has to, and his jobs may have been of a certain type. If you do little more than write prescriptions, the patient's inner life, or the doctor's, doesn't matter very much. There isn't time to find out about it. Even if he has got worse, he'll know the system well enough to pervert it without setting off too many alarms."

"That's what he's done here. But if he feels that his life is in decline, I warn you, he'll try to take you down with him."

*

On route to The Belair to collect his mail and the list of new supervisees, Avalon called ahead to make sure it would be ready.

"It's Dr. Avalon," said Cobb's secretary, receiving the call.

"How shall we handle it? Avalon is on his way in."

"Send him to the training office," said Mendelson, who had stopped into the office for a word with Cobb. "I saw our new man, Prendergast, sitting at a desk there, and I hear he's a tough interviewer. Let him know what's needed; he'll deal with it."

"Good enough. Should one of us speak to Avalon?" asked Mendelson. "He's been at The Belair a long time."

"I know what you mean; do you want to?"

The question fell stillborn to the floor.

*

Prendergast was told what was required and told that Avalon was would be in presently.

"Do you mind taking on an unpleasant task like that?

Prendergast assured them that he was, and managed not to betray the pleasure with which he anticipated it.

"Dottie," Prendergast said to the secretary as he stepped into the reception room of the training office. "Dr. Avalon is coming. Be a good girl and ask him to wait in my office, but don't mention my name."

When Avalon arrived, Dottie said dutifully, "Good morning, Dr. Avalon. Go right in. You may have to wait just a little while."

"What is it?" He had never been asked to wait like this before, and had no idea of what he was waiting for.

"I don't know, Dr. Avalon. They asked me to tell you that."

She left before Avalon could ask another question. Avalon went into the office and waited, unaware that the desk in front of him was Prendergast's.

The phone on the desk rang, and continued to ring.

"You!' said Avalon, when Prendergast appeared in the doorway.

"Why didn't you answer the phone?" Prendergast demanded. "You must have heard it ringing."

"I didn't think that I ought to answer your phone any more than you should come onto my property."

"You don't know the first thing about how people should interact. It's just as well the hospital has decided to let you go."

"Who told you that?"

"*I'm* telling *you* that."

"On whose authority?"

"Mine."

"I was hoping to speak to Mendelson, or Cobb."

"If you can. Be my guest. Has your wife finished moving out?" Prendergast flounced out of the room as if he were in a hurry to get somewhere else.

From another office down the corridor, one that was empty, Prendergast called his office again. Avalon extended his hand towards the ringing phone, then drew it back. It occurred to him that Prendergast might be calling his own office again in the hope that he, Avalon, was still in it, and to see if he picked up. It was not too dissimilar from the sort of thing he did on Adams Street.

"I can't always deal with things as if I were at home and he was acting up next door," he thought, and lifted the receiver.

"Why are you answering my phone?" asked Prendergast, barging in.

For a moment Avalon tried to remain silent, then said, "Why are you calling yourself?"

Prendergast absorbed Avalon's answer. He would bide his time until the opportunity presented itself for a reprisal. Once aroused, Prendergast's passion for revenge was slow burning and not easily exhausted. As a fundamental appetite it had its fluctuations. Prendergast was, in one respect at least a patient man, willing to live with revenge, to derive his inspiration and his warmth from it.

"Is Avalon still in your office," said Cobb, running into Prendergast on the way to the canteen.

"Perhaps he fancies he can stay there. He has a poor sense of boundaries. When he was waiting for me there he answered my phone."

"Did he do that?"

42

Mrs. Marston's complaint against Prendergast to the Licensing Board for Mental Health Professionals also named the Middlesex Hospital. At a meeting of The Board, Dr. Lee wondered aloud if there might recently have been some slippage in the quality of the hospital's permanent staff. The Board dispatched Dr. Lee to investigate.

There was little on paper to account for any deterioration of standards. The office support staff was unlikely to have had much of an effect on things. He would begin his inquiry with Angelo, who had recently been hired as a mental health worker.

His investigation of Angelo began sooner than he anticipated. At a side entrance to the hospital he noticed Angelo, without knowing who he was, and another youth huddled close to each other, talking in low voices. There was nothing unusual in this; hospitalized youth, as they got better, were allowed increasing liberties and frequently gathered around the entrances to the hospital. Lee passed them on the way in. Told at the personnel office that Angelo had gone outside for a smoke and was most likely one of the two by the door, Lee got his description and returned to the door by which he'd entered, just in time to see the patient with whom Angelo had been talking put something in his pocket and slip by Lee on his way indoors back to his unit.

"Are you Angelo?" Lee asked.

Angelo nodded.

"I'm Dr. Lee."

A capacity for being diplomatic was a quality that Dr. Lee was proud to attribute to himself except when a just cause or one of his principles was involved. The scene at the door bore every sign of a drug deal, the sort of thing Lee's principles obliged him to abhor and take action against. He might have gone back in and brought the matter to the attention of the hospital administration, but he was pressed for time, and Angelo was only a mental health aide.

"If you're dealing here, it has to stop." Lee moved closer. "Empty your pockets."

It was a mistake to speak in a peremptory manner to Angelo and expect to be obeyed. As Dr. Lee drew close, Angelo drew closer and maneuvered him against the wall. An older youth in his neighborhood had taught him how to keep the blade of a knife horizontal so that it would be more likely to slip between the ribs. The situation at the hospital side door with Dr. Lee might give him a chance to put what he had learned into practice: he pressed the point of the blade against Dr. Lee's shirt.

"Ha! Gefühlsarmut!" Dr. Lee cried out in the first moment before he fully grasped what was happening to him. Absurd as it was, it broke the sequence of feeling and action in Angelo so that he changed course and held out his free hand. Dr. Lee had by this time collected himself enough to understand that he was being robbed. He emptied his pockets and deposited their contents in Angelo's extended hand, then fell back against the wall as Angelo pushed him, his face torn between the pain of the impact and a smile of satisfaction at having nailed Angelo's diagnosis – a smile that appeared whenever he was pleased with his opinion in a professional matter and felt certain of it.

Before leaving the doorway, Angelo gave Lee another shove. As he fell Lee's grimaced smile lasted another half-second until the ground, brutish and insulting, rose up and smacked him hard in the face.

In the hospital, Angelo went back upstairs to the nurses' station, which had been left unmanned, and emptied into his pockets a drawer of money and other valuables checked by patients when they were first admitted to the ward. He left the hospital quickly by another side door at the other end of the hospital from where he had left Dr. Lee lying on the ground.

Angelo had never thought of his position at the Middlesex as permanent. He had received the week's paycheck earlier that morning. Now was as good a time to leave as any. Always practical, he had given the hospital a cousin's identity when he was hired. Now he had to move on so that the suspicions that would inevitably be generated by the afternoon's events would not catch up with him. And now that he had lost a steady source of revenue, he needed extra cash.

An ad in a local throwaway offered fifty dollars to those who volunteered as subjects in a scientific experiment.

*

When Waring returned to his lab from his typically hasty lunch, Angelo, wearing his black leather jacket, his straight black hair smoothed back, leaned against the doorjamb waiting for him.

"Dr. Waring?"

"Are you here for the experiment?"

"The ad said subjects are paid fifty dollars."

"That's right."

"Up front?"

". . . All right. What's your name?"

"Angelo."

"You'll have to give me some information first and sign a consent form."

"Okay."

Waring gave him fifty dollars from the roll in his pocket; Angelo followed him in.

While Angelo watched a film in which a nineteen-year-old planned and executed a nasty revenge on a boy who had insulted him, Waring looked over the images of Angelo's brain activity before, during and after the film.

"What's this experiment about?" Angelo asked, after the apparatus was detached from him.

"I can tell you now. We're studying brain activity when a person is focused on revenge. We find that the pattern of brain activity when a person is enjoying revenge and when he is eating a good meal is remarkably similar. The way people eat these days, revenge might be better for your health.

Glancing again at the images of Angelo's brain activity before and after the film, Waring asked with a knowing smile.

"You ate just before coming here, didn't you?"

"No."

Waring looked surprised, perhaps alarmed. Angelo, casting a cold eye, quietly enjoyed the dismay in Waring's face, where a spasm of worry flickered so briefly that he could let it go without being much aware of it or trying to figure it out.

43

Coming on top of having moved out of the house on Adams Street, the difficulties at the laboratory made it hard for Helena to believe that she belonged there, and left her feeling like a homeless waif. She reached out where she could.

"Henry?"

"Helena! I'm glad you called. How have you been?" The resonant timbre of his voice comforted her.

"I . . ."

"You don't have to answer."

"How have you been?"

"Well enough. I've missed you."

She avoided that. "There have been problems at the lab."

"Shall we talk about it over dinner?"

"I'd rather it be lunch."

"It's good to see you," said Henry when they met in the restaurant. Since Helena had moved out, they were only this close when they met to hand over Freddie from one to the other.

"It's good to see *you*."

"That's good to hear."

"I couldn't think of a way out of the situation at the

house unless I left. I thought we were trapped."

"Things have been happening elsewhere." He brought her up to date on the situation at The Belair.

"You don't actually need the hospital, do you?"

"No, but it's a community of a kind. I'm going to feel it, not being there anymore."

"I can't believe that Prendergast is there."

"He probably looks good enough on paper."

"It's better to create a small cell of sanity in the family, and choose friends regardless of what they look like on paper," said Helena, thinking of the situation at the laboratory where everyone had sterling credentials, but the atmosphere was toxic.

"That's how I've come to see it too. Helena . . .?"

"Yes?"

"Shall we go home?"

"Does home have to be on Adams Street?"

"I've put it up for sale."

"Oh, Henry!"

The way she said it left him uncertain of her feelings; perhaps she regretted his having done something impulsive.

"You never know. Something may yet happen to the creep." Between themselves they no longer used Prendergast's name. "I agree that we can't wait for that, but I still don't think we ought to move precipitously."

"We can test the market."

"It's been put on the market.

"Let's go home now."

They walked with their arm's around each other towards Adams Street.

"It's too bitter that we haven't been able to find a way to get him."

"Would you stay in the house with me if we could?"

"With you; but not in the house. He hasn't been caught yet, and even if the most egregious behavior were to stop, there are all sorts of outrageous behaviors that break no laws, and he'd figure out what they are. I don't want to spend any more time dealing with him, or even trying to understand what's been happening. There's nothing for it but to move."

"Actually, we may have a buyer . . . . You don't look as relieved as I thought you would."

"Do we tell whoever moves into the house after we're gone about the creep?"

"All I know is that it's not a reason not to sell the house."

44

Prendergast was dissatisfied with the tribute that had been written for his farewell ceremony at the Middlesex. It was unworthy of him, a poor reflection of the honor and respect that were due, and written by fools and imbeciles. He decided to re-write it and make it better, and rehearsed the revised and improved voiceover for the Middlesex valedictory with body and voice in front of the mirror.

"Who can fathom the origins of the qualities that make a man stand out among the rest?"

The sound of his own voice mingled confusingly in his ears with a substantial, full-bodied, nasal sound, the same he thought he'd heard so early that morning when he had been too sleepy to find out what it was or where it came from.

Flustered, he interrupted his recital and wondered aloud, "What is that noise?"

It came from outside, from Avalon's house, and was unlike anything he had heard before. It lacked the aggressive, intrusive edge of the sounds he had inflicted on the Avalons. They lacked the warrior's panache that inspired him, and he despised them for it. Trying to pester him with these sounds in the afternoon betrayed a lack of motivation on their part to match his own outrages; he had often sacrificed his own sleep to stay up in the small hours of the morning to maximize the misery. He smiled, anticipating how he might reply to Avalon's pitiful provocation later that night.

There was another principle, besides his conviction that Henry and Helena Avalon were vile people who deserved it, that drove Prendergast to continue to harass them that night and the following. Persistence was a virtue, a masculine virtue. To cease or let up would be a sign of unmanly lassitude. Prendergast's resentment took on added proportions that night.

It was an hour when the raccoons, having emerged from their dens and descended from the trees, were on the prowl; when the neighborhood possum left the foliage at the rear of the Avalons' garden that was darker than any other cover in the vicinity, to forage.

"Hum-m-m-m-m-m-m-m-m-m-m-m-m-m-m-m-m-m-m-m. Hum-m-m-m-m-m-m-m-m-m-m-m-m-m-m-m-m-m-m-m. Hum-m-m-m-m-m-m-m-m-m-m-m-m-m-m-m-m-m-m-m."

It was four o'clock. The Hari Krishnas had begun their early morning chant. The raccoons scampered over the garden walls and scattered down the block; the possum, not withstanding his razor-sharp teeth, retreated back into darker shadows.

Unable to go to sleep, fitfully brooding over what he could do and filled with an undischarged rancor he thought was bad for his health, Prendergast went onto the driveway next door with a hammer and ice pick, punctured the tires of their new van, then returned to his bed where he was finally able to go to sleep.

Later that morning he found a bullet hole in the trunk of his new Forester.

*

"Hum-m-m-m-m-m-m-m-m-m-m-m-m-m-m-m-m-m-m-m-m. Hum-m-m-m-m-m-m-m-m-m-m-m-m-m-m-m-m-m-m-m-m. Hum-m-m-m-m-m-m-m-m-m-m-m-m-m-m-m-m-m-m-m."

The chant recurred again later in the day, more aggravating each time Prendergast heard it. The ring of the telephone only added to the annoyance. It was Jeremy Smith, chair of the city Zoning Board, calling to let Prendergast know that he had bought the house next door.

"You're living there now?" Prendergast asked in disbelief.

"Da-da-da-da . . . da-da-da-da . . ."

"No. We're not closing on the property for several months yet. Avalon had already rented it to some religious group. He says they're a bit pasty-faced, but a peaceful, harmless lot."

"Da-da-da-da . . . da-da-da-da . . ."

"Are they going to be there long? They do a lot of chanting at odd hours."

"Hum-m-m-m-m-m-m-m-m-m-m-m-m-m-m-m-m-m-m-m-m. Hum-m-m-m-m-m-m-m-m-m-m-m-m-m-m-m-m-m-m-m-m. Hum-m-m-m-m-m-m-m-m-m-m-m-m-m-m-m-m-m-m-m."

"A year at least – I won't be living there. I agreed to honor the lease they signed with Avalon, until they find a permanent structure. Meanwhile, the house on Adams Street will be their temple. Avalon gave me a significant discount on the selling price because of these complications – made it well worth my while to buy it. He's been surprisingly helpful doing what's necessary to clear it all with the Zoning Board.

As territorial as any of the four-legged creatures in

the neighborhood, Prendergast went outside to inspect the length of the property line where he found the spent cartridge of the bullet that had put the hole in the trunk of his car. He hesitated to call the police. There was no knowing now just how fervent or aggressive, even violent, his new neighbors might be.

The changes next door gave a new urgency to what he communicated in a follow-up message to Jeremy Smith at bedtime.

"I believe you understand what's right. At least you did when you chaired the meeting of the zoning board," he e-mailed. "I doubt that I'll run into the same problems all over again when it comes to your building an appropriate fence along our joint property line, with eight feet of flat board and two feet of lattice on top. I should be able to contribute something."

"Hum-m-m-m-m-m-m-m-m-m-m-m-m-m-m-m-m-m-m. Hum-m-m-m-m-m-m-m-m-m-m-m-m-m-m-m-m-m-m. Hum-m-m-m-m-m-m-m-m-m-m-m-m-m-m-m-m-m-m."

The sound went on, insistent, nasal, quivering, soft, invincible.

45

The tribute planned in recognition of Prendergast's years at the Middlesex County Hospital was to take place in the hospital's auditorium. A ten-minute film biography was to be followed by testimonials.

Arthur Winfield, University Professor of Moral Values, who frequently lent himself to civic occasions and ran a program that provided undergraduate volunteers to the local hospitals, would be master of ceremonies. He had a long association with the Middlesex, a public hospital that was always in need of money and barely maintained its university affiliation.

A morbid curiosity, inexplicable to himself, had driven Avalon to go. People were gathering in the auditorium, milling about nibbling snacks and chatting. It was easy to slip in. Passing by the projection room on his way to a seat, Avalon looked twice at the projectionist standing by the door. It was his patient, Geoffrey Parsons, one of Winfield's volunteers.

Avalon saw Parson's open, friendly face today as he had not quite seen it before.

"Dr. Avalon! I didn't know you'd be here. I'm glad you are. I've always wanted to do something to show you how much I appreciate all you've done for me. Today I can do that. "

"How do you mean?"

"I've worked an entire month researching and putting together what you're going to see."

"But what's it got to do with me?"

"Sometimes you just have to wait and see. I've learned that from you," he said evasively with the smile of an accomplice. Avalon replied with a hesitant smile of his own.

The Middlesex was a community hospital whose staff had humbler aspirations, but were more likely than in the grand hospitals across the river in Boston to put together an event to commemorate a staff member's departure. The mental health and social workers, urged to attend by the unit chiefs, had been careful not to risk incurring their displeasure by not showing up; they appreciated the free snacks.

Prendergast forgot about his new neighbors as he looked around the auditorium – the flowers at the front of the room, the snacks and drinks laid out on a table covered by a long roll of white paper, the respectful whispers of the audience waiting for the tribute to begin. It was gratifying to see that the auditorium was full.

Important people were there: Mendelson and Cobb had chosen to grace the event with their presence. Prendergast nodded his head in approval. Such a display of honor and respect was a personal triumph. This recognition by his profession and the staff at the Middlesex, to be followed by advancement to a more prestigious hospital, elicited a rare smile not bought at the cost of someone else's pain or humiliation, a smile of enjoyment in a man for whom pleasure was seldom a goal.

The translucent windows did not allow views of the greenery outside; the attention of the audience would be where Prendergast wanted it – on himself. The chatter subsided and excitement stirred in the audience as the lights dimmed. In a halo of light on the screen appeared the words:

A Fond Farewell
to
Albert Prendergast, MD.

A narrator's voice intoned: *"Who can fathom where the qualities come from that make a man stand out among the rest?" Born a Baltimoron, Albert was the first in his family to attend university. He displayed drive and ambition early, even in his relations with his siblings."*

The screen at the front of the auditorium showed an enlarged black-and-white snapshot in which the boy Prendergast stood above a smaller boy who lay prostrate on the ground with Prendergast's foot on his back.

"Early struggles did not stop his advance in life."

A hesitant laughter rippled across the room. In the next still a twenty-two year old Prendergast in cap and gown, his eyes already concealed in deep shadows beneath his brow, scowled back at the camera. Whoever had taken the photograph could not have enjoyed what he saw through the viewfinder.

The screen went dark as night as Parsons left the old stills behind. Tremolo had pursued his interest for years and the quality of his material was surprisingly good. There on the screen in the middle of the night were the two houses across from the park on Adams Street.

"Albert Prendergast has always believed," the narrator continued, *"that his purpose as a physician was to manage others' conditions so that they could live in peace, free of the aggravation and fear that **so** often accompany and produce ill-health."*

On the screen, dressed in his nightclothes, Prendergast stood on his balcony emitting a loud, penetrating, angry whistle that would have sent the most loyal pet running the other way.

It was followed by repeated renditions of the shrill call of the night that lacked any trace of melody or rhythm, and was so excruciatingly familiar to Avalon.

There was a stir and nervous laughter while some in the audience held onto the notion what they had seen so far was a kind of joke, a bit of a roast perhaps, meant to be funny.

"Dr. Prendergast ," the narrator resumed, *"has been tenacious and persistent in all his pursuits . . ."*

The audience watched Prendergast venture in the dead of night onto the Avalons' driveway holding an axe with which he struck the roof and one of the doors of the car parked there. Returning to his own driveway, he slammed the door of his car repeatedly, rattled the lid of an iron trash bin, blew his car horn, and whistled shrilly, first in his driveway, then, a minute later, half undressed, from his balcony, bending backwards and forwards like a singer throwing everything he's got into his performance.

"He can always be counted on to get the job done."

In a scene from another night Prendergast, wearing a sport jacket against the evening chill, bent over

Avalon's car and drove an ice pick into the left rear tire.

The audience's reaction was louder now, and less articulate, as confused laughter gave way to shouts and gasps.

"His concern for others motivated him for years to forgo the higher salaries in better funded private institutions and devote his time to the patients at Middlesex."

Prendergast was having none of it. His rage was all he had to shore up against disaster. A picture of a younger Prendergast from the year he began at The Middlesex flickered on the screen while he ran to the back of the auditorium, but the door to the projection room was locked. Parsons did not respond when Prendergast banged on it.

"Stop this! Stop it! Open the door, you faggot!"

His shouts were no more effective than the blows on the door. Prendergast remained captive at his own show.

A career that employees and colleagues had come there to honor, and had been put together over many years, was over. Mendelson and Cobb, accomplished at climbing ladders, understood this at once. Choosing not to stick around for its anti-climax, they exchanged glances and waited for a moment when the screen darkened again. With a quick, secure sense of what was good for professional survival, they slipped out of the auditorium.

"I don't know that this will blow over," Cobb said, as he pushed open the doors.

"I've always thought there was something odd about him."

"I can't say I ever really liked him myself."

"Anyhow, we have grounds for not keeping him on now. He's hardly in a position to protest."

Avalon looked around the stunned audience and imagined what was going on in their minds as they witnessed the exposé. In the back of the auditorium Angelo no doubt saw an opportunity to blackmail Prendergast and extort more prescriptions from him. Lee would reflect, with a feeling of triumph, on how widespread ADS was and how it showed up in the most unlikely places. One saw in the pale faces of the well-intentioned mediators that they were suffering an unbearable embarrassment and were on the verge of walking out. Waring, always on the lookout for a new research topic to advance his career, left half amused, thinking it would be interesting to scan Prendergast's brain. Arthur Winfield, Professor of Moral Values, suspecting there were none, just slipped away.

Many did not leave; the show was too good, too rare.

Insight? Revenge? Justice? Mere fantasy? How was Avalon to distinguish what was happening from what he only imagined? There are times when one's imagination is more than mere fantasy.

Above the audience, looming larger than life on the screen, Prendergast was on his balcony again, howling and whistling shrilly, loudly. Prendergast's screams and shouts at the door of the projection room mingled and became confused with the howls and piercing noises on the screen. The steel bent, but the lock held. Safe behind the projection room door, Parsons kept the show running.

Someone had called hospital security. They made their way into the auditorium, seized Prendergast by the arms to stop his assault on the projection room door, and tried to drag him out. Prendergast would not go gently, and security called for back-up. First the sound of a police siren pierced the auditorium's translucent windows, then the blinking blue light of a cruiser.

46

It was the sweetest time that Henry had had with Helena and Freddie in months, too sweet to spoil it by crowding it with activity. Relieved of the oppressive situation having to live next door to Prendergast, they said little, did less, and loved every minute and each other.

Ghosts may not exist, yet people haunt us. A month or so passed, and then it struck Avalon that he had not heard a word about Prendergast despite the drama of his public disgrace.

A discreet call to the Board confirmed that Prendergast still had his license – Avalon, after all, had not been his patient. Nor was his name on any court docket. When Henry and Helena met with Timothy White to deal with the conveyance of documents pertaining to the purchase of their new property, Prendergast came up like a phantom pain still felt after the diseased tissue has been removed.

"I've never felt about anyone else the way I have about Prendergast," said Helena. "I was never much interested in justice before, not for anyone in particular, and I don't usually walk around and go to sleep longing for justice, but I do when I think of him. It's like a hunger I can't get rid of even when I'm tired." Henry nodded.

"I don't understand, after what's been made public, how he can still be in practice?"

"You're not living next to him any more," said White, ever the conciliator when he could be. "You've got that."

"We've got him too, with that film footage," Henry said with a satisfied, easygoing, low-pitched voice *à la papa*.

"Are you sure?"

"How do you mean?"

"From the legal point of view it's a question of evidence."

"We've *got* the evidence now!"

"Evidence isn't always admissible, not even good evidence."

Neither Henry nor Helena said a word. Confusion and an unextinguished dread kept them silent. Like the grey dawn of a vile day, what Timothy White had said glimmered at the edge of Henry's consciousness.

"Not all evidence is admissible," White repeated himself. "You can't use what someone says on the telephone in court, for example, unless the police first got a warrant to tap the phone. He may hire a lawyer too and make a comeback of sorts."

"Like a monster in a sci-fi you mistakenly think you've finished off." Helena did not look amused.

"He could still put up a fight if he has a reasonably good lawyer working for him. It would have to be someone young who doesn't know Prendergast's reputation for not paying bills."

"But we've got him on film. People saw it!"

"It was a good show, but not necessarily the last act. He'll say he's a naive victim driven to what he did by your treatment of him, that *he* never thought to film the things *you've* done to *him*. Are you sure you want to continue this fight with him? You've left his orbit now, if you leave well enough alone. Why not be content with that?"

Helena stared into the space in front of her.

"You're not saying that you're sure the evidence is inadmissible, just that it *might* be, right?" said Henry. He couldn't let it go. "What are the odds that we'd ever get some justice?"

"Justice? How much justice can you afford?"